DIRTY DADDY

SINNERS WELCOME

SAMANTHA BARRETT

For my Books And Bitches girlies, especially Skye Gordon, this one is for you ladies because I just know how much you all love shrimping...
It's easier to ask for forgiveness than permission...

Don't ever agree to drive eight hours in the freaking snow to meet your best friend's future in-laws! I lost cell service about an hour ago and my phone is nearly dead. I've never gone camping, road tripping or even left my fucking hometown until I applied for Brown and got accepted. Living in Rhode Island has been... an experience. I come from a small town where everyone knows everybody's business and they all go to church every Sunday and praise God.

That was never where I wanted to spend the rest of my life.

I've always had this restless need to escape the confines of that town and get out into the world. It's weird to explain, but I can just feel within myself that there is something more out there for me. I'm not destined to marry the boy I have known my whole life and went to school with like my mom wants. She was fucking livid when I told her I was moving. I haven't spoken to her since I left. I'm majoring in English Lit. I want to be a writer.

I was born to be one!

I grip the steering wheel and lean forward, trying to see out the windshield better as the snow continues to fall without mercy. It's starting to get dark and I'm worried I'm lost, but the GPS says to keep heading straight for another three miles and my destination will be on the right. I haven't seen any other mailboxes or cars for at least forty minutes.

I spot the driveway up ahead and sigh with relief. I pull in but stop when my phone begins to ping with notifications. I could weep at finally having service again. I put the car in park and bring up my chat with Peyton.

PEY

We're running late!

We're on the way.

Why aren't you replying?

Tess?????

We can't get through!

The roads are closed.

Tess? I'm worried, where are you?

Van just told me that you won't have cell service until you reach the cabin. The roads are closed because of the snow. Me and the guys can't get through. I hope you get this before you get there.

"What the fuck?" I breathe out as I begin to type out a reply.

ME

I just pulled into the driveway!

PEY

Oh my God!

Finally you reply.

ME

-What the hell am I supposed to do now?

My phone begins to ring with an incoming call, I answer and bring it to my ear.

"Peyton, what the hell do I do?" I hiss.

"Tess, I'm so sorry. I don't know what else to say, I didn't think the weather would turn this fast!" I scrub a hand down my face, this is what I get for having anxiety and always needing to be fucking early instead of late!

"Pey, I'm sitting at the end of the driveway. The snow is falling faster and it's nearly dark," I whine. I'm not mad at her, I'm just pissed I'm in this situation because of my damn self.

"Hang on, Van wants to talk to you." Before I can protest, Van's voice comes through the speaker.

"Tess?"

I smirk. "Priest." He growls, causing me to chuckle.

"My dad and brothers will put you up until the roads open again." His gruff tone suggests he isn't exactly thrilled about this idea either.

"I'd rather sleep in my car," I mutter.

"If you want to freeze to death, then be my guest, but I can assure you, they already know you're there." My eyes widen at his declaration.

"How?" I screech.

"They live in the middle of nowhere, Tess. They have sensors and cameras set up around the property so they can track prey to hunt. The roads should be open tomorrow. Spend the night there and we should be able to make it up in the morning." Van isn't one for chit-chat so the asshole ends the call without allowing me to speak to Peyton. Resigned to my fate, I pull up my message thread with the guy I've been speaking to online. We've been texting for a couple months and FaceTime every day. He's older than me and a single father. I never thought I would be into the whole *daddy kink* but here we are. We had planned to meet up over winter break but it seems we both have other plans. Clayton has family visiting and I promised Peyton I would accompany her and the guys here, so we had to reschedule.

ME

> So, I have shit cell service and if you don't hear from me in the next twenty-four hours send help! I'm spending the night alone with my friend's future in-laws and I can already picture them being creeps and unsocialized with the opposite sex.

I drop him a pin on my location and wait for his reply. I wait five minutes but still the three dots never appear. My attention is snagged when I see a light flick on in the cabin up ahead. When the front door opens I sigh, knowing I have no other choice but to bite the bullet and drive the remainder of the way. I drop my phone onto my lap and put the car in drive. Awkward doesn't even begin to describe how I feel about this situation. I'm not a people person and I tend to stick to myself.

I refuse to look at the person on the porch as I park my car, then exhale a long breath as I kill the engine. I take a single moment to myself before I garner the courage to step out. The instant I do the frigid air slaps against my cheeks. I cross my arms over my chest and slowly lift my head to finally look at the person.

What in the seven fucking hells!

"Tess?" His gravelly tone washes over me. The sight of him standing there in the flesh, wearing a pair of dark wash jeans and a flannel, long-sleeve shirt giving off that classic lumberjack vibe, sends tingles down my spine. The beard I spent many nights envisioning running my fingers through is right there. His striking blue eyes are wide with surprise, his black hair with tinges of gray slicked back.

My mouth pops open as my shock slowly ebbs

away. I open my mouth to say something, but all that escapes is an ear-piercing scream. He covers his ears with his hands as the front door swings open and two guys come to stand beside him with varying looks of worry. My head begins to spin and my vision turns blurry as my world starts spinning on its axis.

"Shit, she's gonna pass out," I hear someone growl a second before everything turns black.

Kaiden rushes down the stairs just in time to catch her before she hits the snow as she blacks out. I still can't wrap my fucking head around her being *here*!

Tyler whistles through his teeth, snapping me out of my downward spiral. "She is fucking gorgeous." Jealousy surges inside me. I grind my teeth and force my face to remain stoic and not bite my son's head off for finding a girl his own age attractive.

"Carry her in," I say to Kaiden. "Tyler, grab her bags," I bark as I turn and stalk inside the house, trying to wrap my head around what the hell I'm going to do. I was never meant to message her when we matched on that stupid app, she was the one who reached out to me first. I planned to ignore her message and forget all about it, but I couldn't resist and we've been talking for months. We were supposed to meet for the first time over the winter break but then Van called and told me he was bringing his girl home. I haven't seen my son for years, so of course I pushed our plans to accommodate him, his friends and their girlfriend. I just didn't expect Tess to show up here.

"Where do I put her?" Kaiden asks. I whirl around and narrow my eyes.

"She isn't a fucking toy, Kaiden, she's a person," I snap.

He just shrugs, Tess clutched against his chest. The sight of her wrapped in his arms has me clenching my fists at my sides. We've not only Face-Timed every night, we've seen parts of each other that I wish I wasn't picturing right fucking now.

"Put her on the couch," Tyler says as he kicks the door closed behind himself, both her bags clutched in his hands. Kaiden obeys without complaint and lays her down gently. Needing something to do to distract myself, I move around the sofa and toss another log into the fire. "Who the hell is she?"

I face both my sons and find their gazes laser focused on Tess, who is laying on the sofa looking like a sleeping angel. Those luscious plump lips that

I have spent many nights picturing wrapped around my cock are slightly parted. Her long lashes are resting on her cheeks, her hair fanned out around her like a halo of darkness. The phone camera from our FaceTimes didn't do her justice, she is more beautiful in person.

"I'm guessing she is the best friend of your brother's girlfriend," I lie.

"I'm dying to see what Van's girl looks like," Kaiden adds with a devilish smirk. Tyler turns to him and raises his brows in mischief. I sigh and scrub a hand down my face.

"Van will cave both your heads in if you so much as look at his girl wrong. You know he's a territorial bastard," I say. Both of them laugh. I bite back my growl, knowing that this is typical for the three of them. Kaiden is the oldest out of the three, Van is the middle child and Tyler is the youngest.

"Oh, I plan on rubbing baby bro the wrong way," Kaiden says, making Tyler laugh. I shake my head at my sons. This break is not going how I planned and I can only imagine what Van is going to say when he finds out I've been having phone sex with his girlfriend's best friend!

"Hmmm." I snap my gaze to Tess as she begins to stir on the couch, both the boys remaining silent as they focus on the raven-haired minx who has plagued my thoughts every night for months. Tess may look like a fallen angel, but the girl has the mouth of the devil and enough filthy wants to rival a BDSM club. The things she has begged me to do to her when we finally meet would have a priest blushing. Her eyes slowly blink open. My breath hitches and lodges in my throat as I wait. She keeps her gaze focused on the ceiling as her body stiffens. I watch with rapt attention as her chest slowly rises but doesn't fall for a couple of seconds.

She darts her tongue out to moisten her lips and I find myself biting back a groan. She sits up but keeps her gaze straight ahead. My heart pounds against my ribcage as she throws her legs over the side and slowly turns, her eyes locking with mine. All the air rushes out of me when I don't see anger in the depths of those intoxicating green eyes—I see *need*.

"Hi, Clayton," she says quietly. Both my boys snap their heads toward me, but I ignore them as I smirk at the beauty on my sofa.

I stuff my hands in my pockets and smile slowly. "Hello, little minx." Her eyes round. I don't miss the way she subtly clenches her thighs or how her hands grip the cushions of the sofa. The tension in the room is charged with something other than unease now, there is the distinct scent of sexual need pulsing between us. Her being stuck here with me for the next couple of weeks is going to end badly for her pussy, because there is no way I'm not going to sink my cock inside that beautiful pierced, little pink cunt. Seeing it on FaceTime drove me insane with need.

Yeah, she has her hood pierced and that shit drives me mad.

"You two know each other?" Tyler rasps out, clearly surprised by this revelation. I raise a brow at Tess, prompting her to answer. She nibbles the corner of her lip, debating how to respond. She releases her lip and pushes her tongue into her cheek and faces my sons. The moment she takes them in her eyes widen.

Her mouth parts in a silent gasp. "I... holy shit," she breathes out. Tyler just stares at her with a cocky grin, while Kaiden crosses his arms over his chest, flexing his muscles. Both my boys know they are good looking and aren't above using that to their advantage.

"Cat got your tongue?" Kaiden teases.

She snaps her mouth closed and shakes her head. "I'm Tess," she blurts out.

"I'm Tyler and that's my brother Kaiden. I'd

introduce our dad but it appears you already know him." She sinks her teeth into her bottom lip and nods.

"How?" Kaiden pushes.

She sucks in a sharp breath then pushes to her feet and extends her hand to Tyler who takes it in his own. "I guess we're past being strangers since I've seen your father spill your siblings in his hand."

I choke on my own fucking spit!

Tyler's brows leap to his hairline. Kaiden's jaw hits the fucking floor. Tess turns her head toward me and winks. I shoot the little minx a look that I hope portrays I'm going to punish her for that.

"You've fucked our dad?" Kaiden blurts.

Tess shakes her head. "Not yet," she answers without skipping a beat. I keep my face blank as both my boys snap their heads toward me. I've raised my sons to embrace themselves and who they are without remorse. I've never disciplined them by smacking or hitting, I allowed them to learn from their mistakes and never once judged any of them. I never turned my back on Van when he left. I knew he would go out into the world and find himself and what made him happy. My boys know they can always come home. Tyler and Kaiden aren't like Van, they don't enjoy the company of others. Don't get me wrong, my sons frequent town and sow their wild oats, but they always come home.

"You want to fuck our dad?" Tyler chokes out.

Tess purses her lips. "Would you be opposed to me being your new stepmom?" This fucking girl has a quick wit.

"Yeah, considering I was just picturing all the ways I wanted to bang you when Dad and Tyler crashed for the night," Kaiden says with a smirk.

My brows raise as I stare at Kaiden. I yank my hand free of Tyler's and stand before them, suddenly feeling out of place. I thought my sarcasm would break the ice considering I have been sexting their father for months, but it appears I was fucking wrong.

"Wait, no fair, dude. I want to bang her," Tyler whines, causing my jaw to unhinge.

Clayton groans, drawing all our attention to him. He shakes his head at both his sons. "She isn't a fucking toy, you can't declare her off limits—"

"I call dibs!" Tyler shouts, cutting his father off. I look at both of them and damn, they are fucking hot. Kaiden is huge, well over a foot taller than me. His shaggy blond hair is a mess atop his head. His brown eyes are filled with a challenge as he stares down at me. It's freezing yet he stands there in a thin cotton shirt and gray sweats. Tyler looks like a trouble-maker, his brown eyes filled with youthfulness. His brown hair is cropped short on the sides but just long enough on top to skim your fingers through it. He's dressed in similar colored jeans to Clayton but he wears a hoodie instead of a flannel.

"No fair!" Kaiden snaps. When Clayton growls, I turn to face him. He looks like he is two seconds away from smacking both his son's heads together. I drink the sight of their daddy and begin to heat when his blue eyes lock with mine. It's so wrong to want him, but I fucking bet my first born that fucking him would be like nothing I have ever experienced before. He looks like a man who knows how to please his woman and goddammit, I want him. It's wrong because he's Van's father, but I mean, can Van really judge when his own girlfriend is fucking her step-brother?

"Both of you boys need to get the hell out of here. Take Tess's bags to her room. Supper will be ready in half an hour. Go finish your tasks." Tyler and Kaiden both grumble. From what I have learned from Peyton, Kaiden is twenty-seven and Tyler is twenty-three. They may be grown men but they still listen to their father. Both of the guys shoot me a wink as they carry my bags upstairs, leaving me alone with their daddy.

I slowly turn and face Clayton, the hunger I see in his eyes has my pussy clenching on air. I fight to keep my face neutral, not wanting to give away the effect he is having on me, but the sly smirk that graces his handsome face tells me I'm failing.

"Still want to show me that piercing, little minx?" I choke on my fucking tongue. Clayton laughs, further enhancing my shame. I quickly get myself under control before shooting him a glare.

Not one to be outdone, I fire back. "I believe your sons just called me off limits to you," I sass. Clayton slowly eats up the space between us until his chest brushes against me, forcing me to crane my neck back to maintain eye contact. Being in a room with those three hulk's made me feel small.

He lifts his hand and runs his fingers through my hair. I bite down on the inside of my cheek to keep from moaning at the feeling of his hands finally on me after so fucking long. He bends until his lips ghost over the shell of my ear.

"I raised my sons to share *all* their toys. I would have thought watching Van has shown you how well he shares with his friends." My jaw unhinges, and without consent a whimper tears out of me, giving away how his words have hit their mark. "Careful, little minx, I may just let my sons fuck you while I watch, since I know for a *fact* being watched is one of your fantasies." He releases me and stalks out of the room while I stand here trying not to crumple to the floor in a heap of messy need. My panties are soaked, my clit is throbbing for release, and now I am praying that the snow doesn't clear so Peyton and the guys won't make it. I would love to spend the next few weeks exploring Van's family without interruptions.

I couldn't sit still, so I decided to take a look around the cabin. The downstairs is spacious and surprisingly homey and clean. Don't get me wrong, they have the cliché antlers on the wall like all hunting cabins, but the massive floor-to-ceiling windows that give you a clear unobscured view of the landscape are stunning. I could sit in this living room for hours and plot my future romance books.

I continue my exploration of the downstairs and find a full bathroom, spare room, laundry, separate dining room and a study. When Van had mentioned that his family lived in a cabin, I expected some rickety old thing with no running water but this place is nothing like I imagined. It's fucking stunning. All the beams look unique and hand planed, the architecture of this place is second to none. I stop in the small hallway that is located between the study and living room and gaze at the photos that line the wall.

There are so many pictures of Van and his brothers, a few of them have Clayton, but I don't see any with their mother. I find myself smiling at a picture of the four of them at some lake, with fishing rods in their hands and large smiles on their faces, they look so happy. The three boys were clearly young, Kaiden looking like he might have been sixteen-ish.

"That one's my favorite." I jump and cover my chest with my hand as I shoot the man himself a glare.

"You scared the hell out of me!" I scold. Kaiden just smirks and shrugs his shoulders.

"My bad." I roll my eyes and go back to looking at the photos.

"Why isn't your mom in any of the pictures?" I find myself blurting out, then I cringe but it's not like I can take the question back.

"She met Dad, got pregnant with Van, then fucked off after he was born." I whirl around and face him with wide eyes.

"What?" He stuffs his hands in his pockets and stares at me like what he just said isn't a big deal. "I thought Tyler was the youngest?"

He nods. "He is."

I frown. "Does he have a different mom to you and Van?" I push.

"Nah, Tyler's parents died when he was three. His old man was a good buddy of Dad's, so we took Tyler in and that's the end of it. Van is my half-brother but blood means nothing to us. Clayton isn't my biological father."

My jaw hits the fucking floor. "What?" I screech, then quickly snap my mouth closed and shoot him a sheepish smile that just has him smiling and shaking his head. A dark sensual look overtakes his features as he slowly leans in until I taste his breath on my tongue.

"The three of us aren't related by blood, so if you wanted to fuck all of us, you could." Kaiden pulls back, shoots me a wink, then turns and walks away like he didn't just drop a bomb on me. These men clearly have no boundaries or reservations on expressing their wants.

My chest constricts. Clayton raised and loved Kaiden and Tyler like his own. Van may be his only biological son but he never once mentioned any of this while we were texting or talking. All he said to me was he had three sons, he's proud of all of them and loves them more than anything. Clayton is a good fucking man and now, knowing what I do about him, my desire to feel his cock inside me has only grown. My panties are soaked, my pussy is aching with the need for release and if I don't control myself, I'm going to take Kaiden up on his offer and allow all three of them to eat me for supper.

Sitting across from Tess as we eat is harder than I thought it would be. I had every intention of leaving Peyton's best friend alone so I didn't start shit with my brother, but the fact she is here on her own, and my brother is nowhere in sight, makes her fair game. I know Tyler wants her and so does Dad. We're a competitive family, none of us will back down.

We all want to fuck her.

I can see it in my dad's eyes and the way he keeps sneaking glances at her. Ty hasn't been able to stop fidgeting since we sat down.

She is the most beautiful fucking creature.

I've been sporting a fucking hard-on since I caught her ass before she hit the snow. She fit in my arms perfectly.

"So, Tess, have you been talking to our dad for a while?" Tyler asks, breaking the silence. Tess swallows her steak audibly and lifts her gaze to my brother. Dad shoots Tyler a warning that he blatantly ignores, Tyler loves to stir up shit.

Tess sets her knife and fork down and sits up straight, darting her gaze between me and Tyler.

"Okay, let's get this over with, shall we?" she grits out. Tyler and I share a loaded look before focusing back on her. Dad laughs, which just annoys the hell out of us since he seems to get what she means and we don't. Tess rolls her eyes and says, "Let me spell it out for you both. Yes, I have been FaceTiming your daddy and having phone sex. Has he seen my pussy? Yes. Has he seen my tits? Also, yes. Now, so we can get rid of all this tension, would you both feel less left out if I showed you both my tits and ass so we can all be grownups for the rest of this trip?"

"Darlin, you whip that pussy out and I'm filling it," I answer, causing her eyes to spark with a challenge.

"Yes, showing us would definitely help us grow up. I vote yes!" Tyler fucking yells from beside me, sounding like an idiot. Tess shoots him a smile. This smile is filled with fondness, almost like she finds him cute or some shit. Tess looks to my dad for guidance. She won't find any help from him. Dad just laughs and sits back in his seat, crossing his arms over his chest, waiting to see what she will do next. When she swings her gaze back to me, I raise a single brow in challenge. Tess grinds her teeth as she pushes back from the table and stands.

Tyler chuckles and slouches back in his chair, then wags his brows at Tess. I can see it in her eyes, she wants one of us to stop her but none of us will. We're all as invested as each other in seeing the beauty beneath the layers of clothes she wears. She grips the hem of her sweater and pulls it over her head, exposing her white long-sleeve cotton shirt beneath. She sucks in a deep breath, then yanks that off as well. All three of us hiss at the sight of her white lacy bra, barely containing her ample tits that are begging for me to sink my teeth into them.

"Fuck..." Tyler rasps out as one of his hands disappears beneath the table. When Tess reaches for the button on her jeans, my breath lodges in my throat and need courses through me as anticipation begins to build. My cock is rock-hard and pushing against my sweats, begging me to set it free and sink inside her tight, wet heat.

She pops the button and slowly peels the zipper down. I suck in a breath through my teeth as I spy the white lace through the opening. She kicks her boots off, then pushes her pants down her legs. Heat courses through me like a tidal wave. She holds her head high as she runs her gaze over each of us, gauging our reactions. Hesitation is clear in her features until she sees all three of us staring at her with ravenous hunger. Her features morph into pure desire as she takes a step back so we can get a full view of her incredible body. She darts her tongue out and moistens her lips before spinning in a circle, causing the three of us to suck in a sharp inhale when her thong-covered ass is shown, but it's the tattoo on her right ass cheek that has all of us fighting to remain seated.

Daddy.

That's what her fucking tattoo says!

When she faces us again, her eyes are glazed with need. "Clear the table, boys, we're having dessert early." Her mouth pops open as she snaps her head toward Dad. The old man just sits there with a hard look on his face. Tyler and I scramble to toss everything on the counter, while her and Dad remain in a stare off until the table is clear of all the dishes. "Get that ass on this table now, little minx," he demands.

Tess swallows and moves to head toward him but

he holds up a hand and flicks his gaze toward me and Tyler. "Huh?" she asks.

His eyes narrow. "You know the drill, no speaking back." She snaps her mouth closed. The three of us have never done anything like this before, only Tyler and I have shared, but the thrill of it is only adding to my need to be inside her. "Get on the table and spread those legs for my sons. I want to watch them eat that dirty little cunt before I finally introduce you to shrimping." My eyes bug out of my head. I know what fucking shrimping is but there is no fucking way I am doing that. But, the lustful look in Tess's eyes is indication enough that my dad has told her about shrimping and she is eager to try it.

Tess obeys. She climbs onto the wooden table and swivels around until she faces me and Tyler. She keeps her knees bent, clearly unsure and slightly uncomfortable. She isn't the only one, this is new for all of us and I'm never one to not try something at least once. I reach out and run my hands along her smooth legs, relishing in the feel of her soft skin beneath my calloused hands. She begins to tremble as I reach her knees and slowly push them apart. She lays her hands flat on the table behind her and stares directly into my eyes with a challenge.

"Show me that pretty pussy, hellion," Tyler urges, making her eyes burn brighter with intensity. Her restraint snaps and she allows me to part her legs. I hiss through my teeth at the sight of the damp patch on her thong. This needy little girl was begging for this and has the nerve to act shy and uncertain. I reach out and run my knuckle against her dampness, loving the sound that escapes her at my touch.

"You ever taken two dicks at once, baby?" I hedge. She nibbles that damn bottom lip and shakes her head. A groan tumbles from my brother, he and I have shared before so this is nothing new to us but for her, this will be an experience and it's one I want to make sure she never forgets. I want her to beg us for it, I need her submission. "Open those legs wider and show my brother how fucking wet you are." She obeys without complaint. I pull the material to the side and suck in a sharp breath at the sight of her glistening, pierced pussy. Unable to hold back any longer, I grip her under her knees and yank her forward to the edge of the table. She gasps in surprise, but it quickly turns into a cry of pleasure when I bend down and slide my tongue through her slick folds, loving the taste of her.

Peaches and cream.

This is a taste I could get addicted to and that is fucking dangerous, she isn't like us. She comes from the city and for someone like her, this place is just somewhere for her to vacation. She bucks her hips, drawing me back to the moment. Tyler reaches out and yanks the cups of her bra down, exposing her full tits, her nipples pebbled and hard, begging to be tasted. My brother obeys their silent demand and wraps his mouth around one while rolling the other between his fingers.

"Oh, fuck," she moans.

"You like my sons' mouths on you, my little minx?" Dad's tone is gruff and filled with longing. I watch as she slowly turns her glazed eyes to my dad and nods. "Use your damn words!" he scolds. Rather than shrinking back at the bite in his tone, she flushes all over and I feel her need on my tongue.

"Yes!" she purrs as Tyler switches sides to pay her other nipple the same amount of attention. She reaches down and grips the back of my head, pulling me harder against her. "Fuck, just like that."

Ty releases her nipple with a wet pop. "Let me taste her." Tess whimpers. I pull back and use the back of my hand to swipe her juices from my chin, then push back from the table. Tyler grins like a kid on Christmas morning as he claims the spot I just vacated.

"Stop." All of us turn to face Dad. "Turn her around, feet on the floor. She's going to blow Kaiden while you eat her ass."

Tyler helps me off the table, my nerves frayed, my body taut with need and anticipation—it's driving me wild. My skin feels so tight, I want to claw at myself to try and ebb the lust running through my veins. I turn and lay my hands flat on the table as Tyler slips in behind me and runs his hands up my back, sending a shiver down my spine. Kaiden rounds the table and stands on the opposite side. I hold his gaze as he tugs his shirt over his head. My breath hitches at the sight of his flexing muscles. The sinister smirk that graces his handsome face sets a fire soaring through my belly. He grips the waistband of his sweats and pushes them down his legs.

My jaw unhinges, he's not wearing boxers!

"Quicker access for me to get in that pussy,

baby," Kaiden answers without me needing to voice my thoughts. His cock springs free and the sight of it has me clamping down on air. I jerk in surprise when fingers brush along my cheek, drawing my attention to Clayton.

"I can't wait to watch them fuck you." His praise bolsters my courage, I've never done anything like this before. This is all new for me and Clayton knows that. I admitted to him on one of our many phone calls that having three men is something I have always wanted to explore, I just never expected it to happen. My blind trust in him makes me feel safe. I can tell that if I was to say *stop* that they would all listen. Tyler grips the waistband of my thong and slowly peels it down my legs as Kaiden climbs onto the table. I'll admit, the sheer size of his dick scares me. I've only ever had sex with one person and the size of his penis was nothing to write home about, it didn't even hurt when he took my virginity, that guy put the *micro* in micro-penis.

Kaiden spreads his legs and shuffles forward, placing his cock in line with my face, I dart my tongue out to moisten my lips. The fact that his bare ass is on the table seconds after my own, is indication enough to me that these guys don't care about eating off the floor if they don't mind asses on their table.

"Suck it," Kaiden snarls—I oblige without complaint. I open my mouth and take him into the back of my throat without gagging—I'm one of the lucky girls who has no gag reflex. Kaiden's groan tells me he approves of this. I feel Tyler kneel down behind me and shiver with need when he blows his hot breath across my sensitive pussy. I cry out around Kaiden as Tyler pushes his tongue inside my tight little asshole, my eyes widening at the strange feeling. This is another first for me, having my ass eaten.

"Does she suck you good?" Clayton asks.

Kaiden growls and thrusts up into my mouth as Tyler slips a finger inside my pussy. "Fuck yes. Her tight, wet little mouth is fucking perfect." The strain in his tone is evident.

"Can I fuck this pussy, hellion?" Tyler asks.

I release Kaiden and peer back at him over my shoulder and meet his gaze. "Yes." Tyler's eyes blaze with lust as he pushes to his feet. Kaiden grips my hair and forces my mouth back to his cock. I place my hands on the tops of his thighs to give myself more leverage to bob up and down on him as I feel the head of Tyler's dick press against my entrance. I can't stop my gaze from seeking out Clayton as Tyler slowly eases inside me. I gurgle around Kaiden as the feeling of him stretching me out to accommodate his dick burns through me. Clayton is reclined in his seat with his cock in his hand, stroking himself as he watches me fuck his sons.

"Fuck, she's so goddamn tight," Tyler growls.

"I'm fucking that pussy next," Kaiden vows, then tangles his fingers in my hair and yanks my head up. I suck in a deep breath as I stare up at him with spit dripping down my chin. "Would you like that, baby? You want my cock inside that pretty little cunt?"

"Yes," I cry out as Tyler slams all the way inside me.

"You like my brother fucking you?" Kaiden purrs, then uses his grip on my hair to force me to nod. "Yeah, you love all of these cocks, don't you?" He forces me to nod again. I can do nothing but pant and moan as Tyler begins to fuck me. "You're gonna be a filthy little whore for our cocks, aren't you?" My eyes widen at his crass words, I've never been spoken to like that before.

"She likes you calling her a whore, her pussy is strangling my dick and she's getting wetter," Tyler announces. Clayton growls his approval as Kaiden forces my mouth back onto him.

"She is going to rock your worlds, boys. Now fuck her slutty little cunt nice and hard," Clayton adds, making tremors ravage my body. I've never been this aroused before. Mix that heady need with their filthy mouths and I'm an atomic bomb ready to explode.

Tyler's grip on my waist turns punishing as he fucks me mercilessly. Kaiden's thrusts are turning hurried. My orgasm is cresting and I can feel it but I've never come during sex before and I don't know how to react.

It's too much!

"Take it," Kaiden growls.

"Let go, hellion, I want that cum covering my dick." I take Kaiden all the way into the back of my throat as I obey Tyler and quit holding off my orgasm. The second it slams into me, a scream filled with primal need tears out of me. It's so loud and drawn out, even with Kaiden's dick in my throat, that I'm certain if they had neighbors, they would have heard me coming. "Yes, hell yes!" Tyler roars as he fucks me harder.

"Fuck!" Kaiden roars, then rips my head back and holds me there, hovering above him as he begins to pump himself with his other hand. "Open your fucking mouth, you dirty little slut." I moan but obey his command. I flick my eyes up to him in time to watch him throw his head back as jets of cum land on my face. I poke my tongue out, needing to taste him. A stream of cum lands on my tongue and I swallow it greedily.

"Oh, fuck yeah, baby. I'm gonna fill this pussy up," Tyler grits out a second before he's roaring out his own release and coming deep inside my tight little cunt.

"Move," Clayton growls. Tyler obeys and steps aside.

"Watch him," Kaiden growls. I peer over my shoulder as Clayton kneels behind me and wraps his lips around my pussy. I cry out when he pushes his tongue inside me, eyes widening when I feel him sucking. My mind is whirling with 'what the hell is happening' until Kaiden releases me and Clayton grips my arm, whirling me around, then gripping my chin and forcing my mouth open. I lock eyes with him as he spits Tyler's cum into my mouth.

"Swallow," he snaps. I do as Clayton demands and swallow every drop. I whimper at the taste and dart my tongue out to capture the small amount that escaped. He surprises me when he swipes his finger across my cheek. "Open." I do as he says and allow him to clean my face of Kaiden's cum and push it into my mouth. "How do my sons taste, minx?"

I open my mouth, trying to find the right words but nothing comes out. Clayton's eyes narrow, I know he hates it when I don't respond. He grabs my waist and lifts me until my ass is perched on the edge of the table and my back is pressed against Kaiden. Clayton steps between my legs and lines his cock up with my entrance, my jaw unhinging as realization crashes into me.

I'm about to fuck their father after I just fucked them.

Clayton gives me no warning as he slams inside me with enough force to shift the table. I throw my head back and scream. I cry out in shock when he slaps my tits, drawing my gaze back to him.

"Eyes on me while my cock is inside this dirty little cunt." My breath lodges in my throat. Kaiden grabs my arms and lifts them to wrap around his neck.

"Keep them there," he growls, turns my head, then captures my lips in a heated kiss that sucks all the air from my lungs. I arch into his touch when he pinches my nipples. The whole wrongness about this entire situation only fuels my hunger for them. I break the kiss when I hear Tyler groan. He stands at the edge of the table with his dick in his hand but his focus is on his father's cock disappearing in and out of me.

"Oh, shit," I cry out when Clayton hits that

sweet spot inside me. After my experience with Tyler, I know if he keeps stroking that spot I'll come again. I dig my nails into the back of Kaiden's neck, causing him to sink his teeth into the side of my throat, drawing a sharp cry from me. Clayton's eyes darken as he lifts my legs and places them over his shoulders. "Holy fuck," I shout when he slams inside me.

"You like that?" Tyler asks.

"Fuck yes, he feels so deep. I need more," I beg.

"You want me to ruin this dirty little cunt, don't you?" Clayton snarls.

I lock eyes with him. "Yes, ruin my greedy cunt for everyone else." Clayton's eyes darken, his grip on my waist turns punishing as he presses forward, forcing me harder against Kaiden. Without over-thinking it, I lean forward and capture *Daddy's* lips in a kiss filled with passion and burning desire. He pulls almost all the way out of me before slamming forward. I scream but he swallows the sound while fucking my mouth with his tongue in sync with his cock. My orgasm rips through me without warning. I arch forward but his body keeps me pressed against Kaiden. Stars dance in the corners of my eyes as I fight to remain conscious. Clayton breaks the kiss. I stare up at him with my mouth open and eyes wide.

He spits in my mouth!

Shock ripples through me until he spits in my mouth again. I close my mouth and swallow, loving the sight of his eyes blazing. He thrusts inside me once more before he comes with my name on his lips. Tyler slides up beside him, forcing Clayton to lean back. He strokes himself twice more before he comes, calling out the name *hellion* and comes on my stomach, marking me.

The thought of the three of them marking me and wanting me like this daily has warmth spreading through me. I could get used to being locked in this cabin with them if it means being fucked like a filthy whore daily.

Wait!

I just fucked Clayton! He's Van's father!

Holy shit, I just fucked Van's father and brothers. Now I'll have to face him tomorrow, knowing that I just violated the very table I'm sure we'll all be sharing meals on.

"Power's out." I turn away from the grill and frown at Kaiden.

"What?"

He rolls his eyes. "We lost power. We're snowed in, brother. Once the gas runs out on the grill we're going old school and cooking over the fire in the living room." I nod, this is nothing new for us. We lose power all the time. "You think Tess is gonna come out of her room anytime soon?"

I shrug. "After I blew my load on her last night she couldn't escape us fast enough." Tess shoved us all away from her and ran up the stairs. I'm man enough to admit I pocketed her thong but put her jeans and shirt in the washer, because I'm a gentleman like that.

"Well, she can't hide in there all day, because the heat is off until the power comes back on." I groan and shoot my brother a look.

"We're all bunking in the living room, aren't we?" Kaiden rubs his hands together and wags his brows.

"Sleepover time, little brother." I close my eyes and groan, Kaiden is the worst to share a room with. The fucker is like a black belt in his sleep and snores. Whenever the power is out we all bring the mattresses into the living room in front of the fire to keep warm. Temperatures drop here suddenly and no amount of blankets will keep you warm, so we always crash in front of the fire when the heat's out.

"Dad eating with us or is he still working?" I ask, changing the subject.

"With the power being out he won't be able to do shit, so yeah." I nod and begin piling food onto the four plates. Kaiden gathers all the condiments and begins setting the table. Now, when I look at that table, all I can think about is her and how perfect she felt, tasted and answered all our needs. She fit each of us perfectly and now I'm left wondering if that was a one off thing or would little Tess be interested in another round of cock hockey?

"You gonna go get her..." I let my sentence trail

off, giving him a chance to go to her himself. Kaiden is shit when it comes to conversations. He relies on his good looks to woo girls, he's never had a girlfriend or ever been interested in dating. He says no girl will ever accept him for the life he chooses to live. He loves being out here and hunting for our food. He hates the city and all the noise. I personally love the solitude our lifestyle affords us.

Kaiden stares at me with a blank look for a second before he shakes his head. "Nah, you go."

I scoff and try to play off his dismissal, I refuse to let him hide away and feel awkward around her. "Nice try, asshole, you're coming with me. I'm not carrying that mattress down the stairs by myself." He works his jaw side to side but says nothing. We finish setting the table in silence before we head upstairs to Tess's room. I rap my knuckles against her door and wait for her to answer, when there is no response after a couple of minutes Kaiden and I share a look, a frown tugging at his features. He lifts his hand and knocks, this time louder.

"Go away!" I bite back my groan when my brother begins smiling, it would have been better for her sake if she remained silent, but now she has just given Kaiden a challenge and he won't back down.

My brother lives to win and if Tess isn't careful, she will become the sole focus of his attention.

"You have three seconds to open this door," Kaiden calls out. "I'm gonna start counting."

"I don't give a shit, leave me alone," she snaps.

"Three!" he calls out, then shoves the door open. Tess jolts upright in bed and clutches the blankets to her chest. Her jaw drops at the sight of us standing in her bedroom. Her eyes are wide with surprise but the moment she darts her gaze between the two of us, her cheeks tinge red, her mind going back to what happened last night. I would be a liar if I said I wasn't sporting a semi just at the sight of her. Tess is fucking gorgeous, she is by far the most stunning woman I have ever met in my life.

"Powers out," I find myself blurting out. Her eyes crinkle at the corners and she tilts her head to the side.

"Ah, okay..." she mutters, clearly confused by my declaration.

"You're about to freeze your tits off in the next hour. The heats out." Tess's eyes widen at Kaiden's declaration. Before either of us can utter another word, she leaps out of the bed, dashes across the room to yank her curtains open and stares out the window.

"Oh, this can't be fucking happening!" she growls. I prowl toward her and press against her back as I stare over the top of her head. She stiffens at my nearness. When she tries to pull away, I grip her waist and anchor her to my front.

"I guess my brother won't be coming after all," I say quietly. Her breath stills and my self-restraint is about to snap. My grip on her tightens, a soft gasp escaping her when she feels my hard cock pressing against her back. "Looks like you're gonna be stuck here... all *alone*... with the three of us."

A tremble works its way down her spine. She pulls free of my hold and presses her back against the window, darting her gaze between me and Kaiden. My brother moves to stand beside me, caging her in.

"I need to call Peyton." Her voice is lined with tension and unease is written across that beautiful face but her eyes, they shine with intrigue and lust. Her mind and body aren't on the same page. Her body wants a repeat of last night, but her mind is telling her that it was wrong and taboo.

"You can try but you won't get any cell service out here, the towers will be down. It looks like you're stuck with us until the snow storm passes and believe me, baby, they can last *weeks*." Her eyes widen.

"You're kidding?" she breathes out.

I shrug. "We never kid about storms out here. Now, how about we carry this mattress downstairs and then eat?" I say.

She shakes her head. "I'll take my chances staying up here," she fires back.

"Not a chance," Kaiden bites out, then stalks over to the bed and lifts the mattress. I gather all the pillows and blankets and shoot her a wink on the way out.

"Breakfast is served, hellion, don't make me come back up and have to fuck some compliance into you." I leave her standing there with her mouth agape and a flush coating her cheeks.

Kaiden and I gather the rest of the bedding from our rooms, then head downstairs. Just as we finish situating the beds in front of the fireplace, Dad comes around the corner as Tess descends the stairs. She pauses a couple of stairs from the landing and stares at Dad. He just shoots her a knowing smirk, then continues into the dining room. We follow after him, leaving her to decide if she will join us or not. We all take our seats at the dining table just as Tess enters the room. She squares her shoulders and holds her chin high as she claims her seat across from us.

"We got enough wood?" Dad asks, breaking the silence as we all dig in.

"Yeah, I'll bring some more in from the wood shed after breakfast before the snow gets too high," Kaiden answers.

"Ty, go and bring in the meat from the outside freezer and we'll store it in here. The news said this is a big blizzard so we'll be stranded for a while." A whimper escapes Tess at my dad's declaration. "You got somewhere to be, minx?" Dad purrs. Tess sits up straight and nibbles on the corner of her lip.

"I didn't anticipate being stuck here this long," she mutters. "I barely packed enough to last the trip as it is," she adds.

"Clothing is always optional," I interject. She shoots me a glare.

"Funny," she mutters.

"Don't act like you don't want to be the meat between our sandwich, baby girl. Last night was just a taste of what you could have." Her cheeks tinge red at Kaiden's admission, eyes taking on a glazed look as if she is reliving memories from the night before.

"Was last night a regret for you?" Dad pushes as he chews a mouthful of eggs.

Tess chokes on her piece of bacon and pounds her fist against her chest. The three of us say nothing, waiting for her reply. She reaches out and grabs her glass of orange juice and downs nearly half the glass.

She looks at each of us, begging for one of us to change the subject but the truth is, we're all wondering the same thing. If she does regret last night it would suck, because she was perfect. She took all of us like a dream and rocked my fucking world. One taste of her will never be enough, her pussy the perfect hole to die in.

"Uh... I... I mean..."

"Use your words, little minx. We're going to be stuck here for a while so I think it's better to make our boundaries clear from the start. If last night is a regret for you..." Dad sighs and slouches back in his chair, appearing relaxed but lines of tension mar his forehead. "That would be a damn shame, Tess, because my boys and I enjoyed fucking ravishing that tight little body of yours, and the thought of not being able to slide inside that pussy again is not something I want to consider."

"I mean, Thanksgiving is coming up and I'm sure my dad would love to slip a straw inside that ass and suck my cum out of you and spit it in your mouth so you get the full effect of *shrimping*." Her eyes widen to the size of dinner plates. Kaiden just stares at her with a vicious smirk on his face. The intrigue is clear as day in her green eyes, she wants to pick up what Kaiden and Dad are selling.

SEVEN

I swallow a couple of times, trying to center myself and get my damn mind out of the gutter. The thought of Clayton sliding a straw inside of me and sucking his sons' cum out has me clenching my thighs together beneath the table. The kink factor with him is real and something I want to explore. My sexual experience may be minimal but I have always had a darker side to me that wants to be set free. Fucking my best friend's father-in-law may not be ethical and is frowned upon, but society is judgmental and vanilla. If Clayton and his two boys are open to a repeat of last night, why am I being hesitant?

These three blew my fucking mind. The way

they gave me everything I have only dreamed of has me soaking my panties.

Fuck it.

Life is hard, we're only here for a short time, not a long one. While I'm snowed in with these three sexy-as-sin alpha males, I may as well enjoy them before I have to go back to school, right?

"I mean, fucking all of you would put a whole a new meaning to *family feast*." Tyler and Kaiden erupt with laughter. I look at Clayton who sits there with a wide smile on his face and shrugs.

"I think KFC should use it as their new ad campaign," Tyler says, earning a chuckle from me. Karma has a weird sense of humor, out of all the men I could have matched with on that dating app, I linked with Van's father. I look at each of them and I can't find it within myself to be mad about this situation. Anticipation begins to unfurl inside me at the prospect of what might happen between the four of us. I'm not stupid, I know this is just sex and nothing could ever come of this.

The guys begin discussing trivial things about their company and I find myself truly interested. It's clear Clayton has worked hard for the fortune he has amassed. Unlike many others who would flash their money around, he doesn't. He lives a frugal lifestyle in the woods with his sons and invests his fortune so he can set his three sons up. Kaiden, Tyler and Van never touched a cent of the money until recently when Van helped his two best friends launch their businesses.

"So, what are you studying at Brown, Tess?" Tyler asks.

I roll my lips over my teeth, debating on how to answer. My family never thought of my chosen career as anything more than a hobby and I begin to worry they will laugh at me. "English Lit. I want to be a writer." I keep my gaze on the table, not wanting to see them laugh at me.

"Why the fuck do you sound so upset about that?" Kaiden snaps.

I flick my gaze to him and frown. "Because it isn't a *real* job," I answer.

Tyler scoffs. "Says who?"

I purse my lips. "My family." Bitterness coats each word.

"Then your family are fools. Literature is a huge part of our history and without the escape books offer us we would have no imagination. Your career choice is noble. Don't let your family's simplemindedness sway you from your dream. If you wake up in the morning and all you can think about is writing, then you, baby...

you are meant to be a writer." I stare, slack-jawed and in awe of these three. I haven't known two of them for more than a day and already I feel a connection developing. Clayton and I have spoken for months and never once have I told him about what I'm studying, but his support of my dream means more than he will know.

Laughter erupts from me when Tyler smacks Kaiden over the back of the head. Kaiden scowls at his brother and tosses his playing cards into the air. "You fucking cheated!" he roars.

Tyler can't contain his laughter and raises his hands in mock surrender. "Dude, you lost, man," he wheezes out.

"You fucking cheated!" Kaiden snaps. He reaches for Tyler but he smacks his hand away, then crawls on his hands and knees across the mattresses we are sitting on, which the boys set up in front of the fire, and hides behind me.

"Did not. You just suck at Uno, man. Not my fault," Tyler defends. Kaiden growls, then launches forward to get to his brother but I'm caught in the middle. His large frame forces us backward, the brunt force knocking the wind out of Tyler, leaving me sandwiched between them. My laughter dies off instantly when Kaiden's eyes lock onto mine. He's nestled between my legs, his brother gasping for air behind me, but neither of us moves as we continue to stare at each other. The room fills with tension and it's not the awkward kind—it's the sexual kind that charges the air.

Need pulses inside me as he slowly lowers his head, giving me every chance to turn away, but I don't. I want this and refuse to deny myself the chance of having all three of them again. This thing has an expiration date and I plan to take advantage of it while it lasts.

When Kaiden's soft lips touch mine, I'm unable to keep my moan from tumbling free, getting louder the instant his tongue swipes mine. His taste overwhelms my senses and I'm nothing but putty in his hands to play with as he pleases. I reach up and wrap my arms around his neck, pulling him in closer. He braces his arms on either side of me. I gasp into his mouth when Tyler shifts beneath me, I forgot about him for a second. I break the kiss and peer back at him as Kaiden licks a trail along my neck, drawing another heady moan from me.

Tyler seizes the opportunity and kisses me, his minty breath overwhelming me. Kaiden grips my shirt, pushes it up and yanks the cups of my bra down. I attempt to break the kiss with Tyler, but he grips my cheek and keeps me in place as Kaiden sucks my nipple into his mouth. I cry out. Tyler swallows the sound and growls his approval at my response. Kaiden releases me with a wet pop and slides down my body. Tyler breaks our kiss and allows me to watch his brother as he grips the waistband of my leggings and peels them down my legs. I sit up and yank my shirt over my head, then toss it to the side as Tyler unclasps my bra and helps me remove it. I shift to push my thong down, but Tyler grips my wrists.

"Nah-uh, hellion, we do this our way and you take what the fuck we give you. Am I clear?" The dominance in his tone sends a shiver of need down my spine. I nod my head.

"Use your fucking words," Kaiden snaps.

"Yes, I'll take whatever you give me." I'm practically panting, my skin ablaze with arousal. Tyler shifts back, then instructs me to get on my hands and knees. I eagerly obey, only to lift my gaze and see

Clayton leaning against the far wall with his arms crossed over his chest and a hungry look in his eyes as he watches us. Tyler pushes his sweats down to free his cock. It smacks against his stomach, rock-hard and leaking with pre-cum. I reach out and grip him in my hand as Kaiden pushes my panties to the side and buries his tongue inside my pussy. I cry out a second before Tyler grips my hair and pushes my mouth onto him. I breathe through my nose as I bob up and down on him.

I spot Clayton out of the corner of my eye, then the bed dips as he drops to his knees beside us. "Hands behind your back," he orders. I follow his demand without question, Tyler's grip on my hair keeping me from falling forward. I gasp around Tyler when I feel the cool metal of the handcuffs slip around my wrists and tighten. My pleasure heightens. Clayton pulls a black silk strip from his pocket and my breathing turns ragged when I realize what it is.

A blindfold.

He ties the material around my eyes. Tyler doesn't quit his thrusting as his father continues to bind the material around my head. The second I lose sight everything becomes heightened. Every touch has me feeling ultra aware, the sounds from the guys and the fireplace seem louder. I'm at their mercy—bound and blind. The notion of being completely helpless has my arousal growing and the need to feel them inside impossible to ignore.

"Here," Clayton says, then I feel Kaiden pull back. I whimper at the loss of his tongue, then Tyler pulls free of my mouth and pushes me back until I'm kneeling. I feel spit dripping down my chin. My nipples are pebbled and hard, begging for their touch but I don't dare utter a word as I wait to see what they will do next. I listen closer and can hear the sound of zippers and their clothes landing on the wooden floor.

Excitement thrums through me when I feel the mattress dip with their weight. I may not be able to see them but I can feel the three of them standing in front of me. I inhale and moan, smelling their musky scent. The fact I don't know which one is which only enhances my need.

"Open that pretty little mouth." I can tell from the slight growl in his voice that it's Tyler speaking. I open my mouth and eagerly wait for it to be filled. The three of them take turns slamming their cocks inside my mouth without mercy. My tears are being absorbed by the blindfold, and the growls of approval coming from them at the sight of me only emboldens my confidence.

"She's a good little whore sucking our cocks, isn't she?" Clayton growls.

"I wonder if her greedy little cunt is drenched?" Kaiden says, that husky lilt gives him away.

"Head down, ass up," Tyler growls. I shuffle forward and rest my cheek against the comforter. "Spread those legs and show us that weeping cunt, hellion." I widen my legs and relish the sound of their groans. I can feel my arousal coating the inside of my thighs.

"I need a taste of that dirty pussy," Clayton growls. I tense in anticipation, waiting for him to make a move. What I don't expect is for one of them to smack my pussy, causing me to jolt forward. I'm horrified when a moan escapes me when they smack it again.

"Would you look at that, the dirty little fuck doll loves getting her cunt spanked." My chest burns as desire rolls through me—it's always been a want of mine to be called a *fuck doll*. I want them to use me. I want them unrestrained and fucking me so hard I can't walk tomorrow. I want the imprints of their cocks ingrained inside me so I can feel the ghost of them for days to come.

I dart my tongue out and slide it through her wet folds. She screams when I suck her clit into my mouth. I bite down enough to apply a slight bit of pain to heighten her awareness. Kaiden moves to the front of her and lays on his back, waiting. I take my time tasting her and inhaling her scent. I release her clit and run my nose through her slit. I want to smell her for the rest of the night.

"You like that, hellion?" Tyler asks.

"Hmmmm, fuck yes," she pants out as I push two fingers inside her tight little cunt. I feel the walls of her pussy shudder around me. She's on the verge of coming and I can't allow that to happen so I pull my fingers free and nod at Tyler. He grips her waist and lifts her, positioning her on top of Kaiden.

"Sink down on my brother's cock slowly, make him work for that dirty little cunt," Tyler growls in her ear. He releases her in time to catch the lube I toss him. The sight of her pussy swallowing my son's cock is euphoric. I grip myself and squeeze, loving it when pain and pleasure are mixed. Kaiden grabs her waist, then thrusts inside her, burying himself balls deep. She throws her head back and screams.

"Oh, fuck!" she shouts.

"Lean forward, this ass is mine," Tyler barks. She shivers and slowly leans forward with the help of Kaiden as Tyler starts lubing up her asshole. My mouth waters knowing it's only a matter of minutes before I get to suck their cum out of her and spit it into her mouth. Shrimping is a kink not a lot of people are into, but I fucking love it. I refuse to use a straw, I love sucking it out on my own. "You gonna take both of us like a good little whore, hellion?" Tyler coos as he slowly breaches her tight muscle wall, forcing a sharp cry from her. When she doesn't answer he smacks her ass twice.

"Use your fucking words!" I snap as I move until I am standing above Kaiden with my dick in my hand.

"Yes. I'll fuck you both so good," she pants out as Tyler continues to ease inside her.

"Mouth open," I command. She sits up and pushes back against Tyler as she opens her mouth. I don't give her a chance to take a full breath before I fill her mouth. She fights against her restraints but it's futile, she'll never get free of those cuffs. When she swirls her tongue along my cock, I throw my head back and groan. "Glide your teeth along it," I grit out. She does as she's told and I shudder at the feeling of her teeth grazing my sensitive flesh. The boys begin to find their rhythm. Tyler cups her tits as he slams into her. The vibration from her groan has me riding the edge of oblivion, but I refuse to cum.

Not yet!

I want my cum inside that wretched little cunt of hers. "Fuck, I'm gonna cum, baby," Kaiden forces out through gritted teeth. I pull free of her mouth and step back. The sight of my boys slamming inside her over and over again has me wanting to bust a nut right here. I stave off my need to explode.

"I'm coming!" Tess screams, her entire body flushing as her orgasm rips through her without remorse. Her cries turn hoarse as aftershocks continue to wrack her tiny body. Kaiden falls over the edge a minute after her, with her name on his lips as he empties everything inside her.

"Fill her pussy, Tyler. I want to triple cream pie

this little slut," I snarl. Tess's lips part in shock. Tyler pulls out of her ass, then lifts her off Kaiden only to force her face into the comforter beside his brother before he's slamming inside her cunt. Tess's screams are like music to my ears. Tyler drags his nails along her bare back, dragging a pain-filled cry from our girl.

"You like that, don't you, you dirty little bitch?" Kaiden snarls.

"Yes. I fucking love it. Fuck me harder, I want to come on each of your cocks!" she yells. Ty's grip on her waist turns punishing as his thrusts harden. Tess comes with such force, her entire body jolts forward, trying to escape Tyler, but he tightens his grip on her as he chases his own release. The second he comes, I dart forward and push him aside so I can fill her before a single drop of their cum escapes her tight, wet hole. "Oh fuck, I can't! It's too much!" she pleads.

"Shut the fuck up and take this dick like a good girl!" I snap as I pull back and slam inside her, hard enough my balls slap against her clit.

"I can't," she pleads in a watery tone. She's wrong. I know she has another orgasm in her and I'm gonna make sure she comes once more before I force her to swallow all of us. She told me she wanted to try shrimping and I refuse to let her off the hook.

Hearing those words come out of her mouth on one of our FaceTime calls fed the monster inside me. I've never met a woman like Tess, her hunger and need for the darker things sex has to offer is one in a million. I won't let this chance to fulfill those desires, of not only mine and hers but of my sons, pass us by.

I reach forward and grip her hair, pulling her up until her back is flush against my front. I sink my teeth into her shoulder. She screams so loud my ears ring but it quickly turns from pain to pleasure as she squeezes the life out of my dick when yet another orgasm slams into her with the force of a hurricane. Two more thrusts and I roar out my release as I fill her pussy with everything I have. I release my hold on her hair. She flops forward, panting and whimpering as I pull out. I flip her onto her back and force her legs apart before pushing my fingers inside her cunt. Kaiden strokes her cheek as Tyler rolls her nipples between his fingers.

I swirl my fingers inside her, making sure to mix our cum together. I pull my fingers free before wrapping my lips around her pussy and sucking our cum out. I slide up her body and grip her chin, applying enough pressure to force her mouth open before I spit our releases into her mouth. I push her mouth closed and watch as she swallows.

"Congratulations, little minx, you just got shrimped." Kaiden and Tyler chuckle and shake their heads. I shoot both my boys a smirk, then gently peel the blindfold off her eyes. She blinks rapidly as she adjusts to the lighting. I hold my breath, waiting to see her reaction. When her green eyes lock onto mine and I see nothing but pure satisfaction and hunger swirling in the depths of those captivating eyes, I sigh in relief.

"Every time we fuck, I want to be blindfolded and cuffed. Being at your mercy was fucking sinister and having no control was the hottest thing I have ever experienced." My brows raise to my hairline, I'm at a loss for words. I took a gamble and hoped she would enjoy it as she had mentioned during our calls that she had wanted to try this.

"Baby, anytime you want to be bound and gagged by dick all you have to do is ask and I'll grant your wish." Tyler snorts at Kaiden and shakes his head. Tess laughs and I find myself smiling. I shift and retrieve the key for the cuffs and release her. She lifts her arms and rubs at her wrists. Guilt churns inside me at the sight of the red marks marring her beautiful skin. When she looks at me, she reaches out and places her hand against my chest, waiting until I meet her gaze before she speaks.

"I'm fine. I loved every second of it and if I wanted to stop or if I was in pain at any time, I would have said something. I wanted this, Clayton." Her words settle the guilt inside me. The soft smile on her face has my chest aching. I knew I had developed feelings for her a long time ago, but I had convinced myself she would be nothing but some chick from the internet who just got off on having the attention of an older guy.

"You may suck at cards and lose every round but at least you won the race from Daddy's sack to Mommy's egg." My lips part in shock as I stare at Tyler. Kaiden crushes the cards in his hands and glares at his brother. Kaiden lurches forward to tackle him as I try to scramble away from them before I get caught in the crossfire but I'm too slow. Hands grip me under my arms and pull me off the mattress. I crane my neck back to see Clayton standing behind me, smiling down at his sons.

"Come on, I'll make you an iced coffee while those two sort out whatever it is they are fighting over this time." The love he has for his sons is clear in his tone, making my chest ache. I wish my family would love me without restraint like Clayton does his boys.

I brush away the thought and follow him into the kitchen. I bite down on my lip to keep from smiling when he pulls out a stool for me at the breakfast counter.

"Such a gentleman," I tease. Clayton places his palms flat on the counter and leans in close enough for his breath to fan across my face as I sit down. I still, his blue eyes holding me captive.

"A gentleman wouldn't fuck you the way I just did." I suck in a sharp breath, stunned silent. I watch as he pulls back and goes about his task of making us some ice coffee since we have no power for hot coffee. I don't know what to say, his comment has rendered me speechless and that's not something that happens often for me. "Stop overthinking everything, Tess." I shake my head and snap my head up to find him staring directly at me.

"I wasn't," I lie.

His brow raises, then he rests his hip against the edge of the counter and crosses his arms over his chest. Fuck. My head immediately goes to the gutter, the sight of him standing there looking like a literal God ready to dole out my punishment has my core clenching.

"What's got you more worried? Is it the fact I'm older or is it that you are fucking not only me but my sons as well?" I swallow audibly, I'm not used to being asked such a direct question like this and I'm fumbling for the right answer.

"I... I mean aren't you?" I clamp my mouth closed and take a deep steadying breath. If I can open my legs for all three of them, I can definitely have this damn conversation like a boss. "It's got nothing to do with you being older." He purses his lips and nods but remains silent as he waits for me to continue. "The fact you are father and *sons* does make me wonder if this is... taboo?"

Clayton snorts right as Tyler groans in pain from the other room. "Of course it's taboo. People say you aren't meant to love more than one person. But, why? Why can't you have more than one?"

I open my mouth to answer but quickly clamp it closed when I realize he's right. Society has programmed us to think we must be monogamous, but why?

"My son loves his girlfriend but does he not share her with his two best friends?" I nod. "He loves her deeply, he gave up his vows as a priest for her. His best friends love her just as much. I believe she loves the three of them equally."

"What are you trying to say, Clay?" I press.

"You're overthinking this whole thing because

you think it's wrong. What if I told you we all think it's right?" My eyes widen to the point they begin to mist with tears, forcing me to blink and absorb his words.

We think it's right.

Clayton abandons making our coffee and moves around the counter, grips the stool and turns me until he is standing between my legs. The heat from his body soaks into me right as his scent overwhelms me. He reaches out and grips the back of my neck, forcing my head back until my gaze meets his.

"Give into this, Tess. We want *you*. My sons have shared before, it may not be right by normal society standards but fuck them. Out here, we can be whoever we want and never have to answer to anyone. I told you months ago, when I want something I go after it and don't stop until I achieve my goal—and I want you, Tess Cohen." Clayton doesn't bother to wait for a response, he seals his lips to mine and short circuits my brain as he devours me with his mouth. Each flick of his tongue is purposeful. Clayton doesn't ask permission, he takes without mercy and forces you out of the bubble you try to live in.

"Dad!" I jerk back at the sound of Kaiden's growl. I peer around Clayton to see both guys standing in the doorway. I expect to see anger or disgust in their features but all I see is lust.

"I knew he would try to cut us out, the greedy bastard." Clayton chuckles at Tyler's declaration.

"I was just warming her up so she would be ready for the fun." My brows draw together in confusion.

"What fun?" I ask looking over each of them, my breath hitches when all their features begin to darken.

"We're snowed in, baby," Kaiden says in a husky tone.

"Nowhere to go," Tyler adds.

"You're trapped," Clayton tacks on. The hairs on the back of my neck stand up as a tinge of fear courses through me.

"I hear you have a bit of a primal kink, baby," Kaiden drawls. My brows hit my hairline as I dart my gaze to Clayton in question.

"You shouldn't have distracted me, little minx, now I won't be able to use my body heat to warm you until later," he taunts.

"Why would I need to be warm?" I push.

"Because you're about to run through the woods in the snow and we're going to hunt you down, hellion." My jaw slackens at Tyler's admission.

"I hope you're good at hide and seek, baby, because when we find you, we're going to fucking destroy that pussy for any other fucker. Those city boys you're used to have nothing on us. We've been taking it easy on you but not tonight. We're going to unleash everything we have on you so be ready to be our little whore." Any normal person would fight against this and try to reason with them that it's too cold out or something like that, but not me. I'm hot all over and the need that is roaring inside me is begging for them to catch me, then fuck me so hard I'll be ruined for anyone else.

If I'm honest with myself, I don't want anyone else. I want this, with them for as long as they will have me, or until reality calls and I have to go back to school. Back to my boring, lonely life.

Excitement rolls through me like waves. It's pushing me to chase her and pulling me back at the same time, so she has enough time to hide. The thrill of the chase has me heating all over—hunting is my favorite thing to do. I'm the best tracker out of the three of us. I know I'll be able to find her within minutes, she's a city girl and I can bet she won't cover her tracks in the snow.

"Man, it's been ten minutes, let's go," Tyler whines from beside me as we stare out the back patio doors into the darkness outside.

"She has on a coat, boots, hat and gloves. She'll be fine," I say in a firm tone. My need for her is riding me so hard that I can barely focus or take a full breath.

"As much as I'd love to fuck her against a tree, we aren't going to do that," Dad says pulling both our focus to him.

"We aren't?" Tyler repeats like a fucking parrot.

Dad shakes his head as he pulls his coat on. "No. We'll bring her back here. The hot tub should still be hot enough even with the power out. We fuck her in there, the last thing we need is to get her sick. Now, get ready, we're about to go catch ourselves a dirty little whore, who needs to be taught a lesson in who she belongs to." A sick sense of ownership flows through me. I love the sound of him saying she is ours. Tess is perfect.

Tyler and I shrug on our coats, then follow Dad out the back. "We using flashlights?" Tyler asks.

I shake my head. "Use the moonlight, keep light on your feet. I want her to think she's won and escaped us." Sinister smirks grace both Dad and Tyler's faces.

"Let's go hunting, boys," Dad declares, then takes off. I tilt my head back and release a howl up at the moon. Ever since we were kids and Dad taught us how to hunt, he instilled in us to never use words if we were separated, but instead howl like a wolf so he could find us. He said speaking would alert predators and make us prey. Tess doesn't know that, so we're all banking on her talking—it isn't the four legged predators she needs to watch out for tonight...

The three of us are spread out, all entering the woods at different points. The moon casts enough light for us to be able to see but not clearly. I don't need clear sight though. Call me crazy, but I feel this pull toward Tess, and I know I'll be able to track her based on that alone. I veer left around some trees and smirk when I see her small footprints in the snow. I release a low howl, alerting the others that I have her trail. I take another step but pause when I hear one of them release a low howl, signaling they have a trail as well. A second later a third howl saturates the air and I whirl around in the direction my dad and Tyler are.

I cut across the dense snow and move toward them, Tyler and I reaching Dad at the same time. "You both caught a trail?" I ask.

"Yeah," they answer in unison.

"How the fuck is that possible? She isn't some girl scout or nature explorer, is she?" I ask Dad.

He scrunches his face and shakes his head. "I don't think so."

Tyler snorts. "You didn't think to ask any personal questions while you were having phone sex?" Dad cuts him an angry glare.

"You're still not big enough to get out of an ass whooping." Tyler and I both laugh, Dad is so full of shit. He has never raised a hand to any of us kids. He likes to threaten us with a whooping because it makes him feel better but we all know he's full of horse shit.

"Split up, we each follow the trails and see where they lead us." I don't wait for them to confirm as I head back to where I was and begin following her trail. Tess told us to give her ten minutes before she ran out the back door into the woods. I'm beginning to wonder if the little devil played us. Before long I run into both Dad and Tyler. The three of us all share a confused look.

"All the trails lead here," Tyler announces.

"No shit, Captain Obvious," I clip out.

Dad narrows his eyes and looks around. His eyes are narrowed slightly but then a slow smile begins to bloom across his face. "It appears *minx* is a fitting name for you after all," he calls out. He drilled into us never to speak in the woods, yet he is shouting and announcing our position to all predators in the vicinity.

"What are you doing?' Tyler hisses.

"She's here." Both Tyler and I reel back and stare at our dad like he's lost his mind.

"Huh?" I press.

Dad looks at both of us. "She tricked us, the trails were a diversion to see if we would chase our tails or actually find her like we promised. Isn't that right, Tess?" he calls out again.

"I mean, I could have been cruel and made extra trails." We all swivel around to the left just as Tess releases the branch of a tree and drops to her feet with a seductive smile on her stunning face. She looks over each of us before crossing her arms over her chest and wagging her brows. "So, since I won, what's my prize?"

"Your prize is our dicks. Now, start running back to the house because when we catch up, you'll be screaming our names," Tyler snarls. She shoots us all a wink before turning on her heel and fleeing back home.

"Fuck. I don't want to let that girl go," Dad admits before taking off after her.

"Neither do I," Tyler mutters before chasing after them.

"Then, we need to make her stay," I mutter aloud, then chase after them. As I break through the woods, Tess's laughter meets my ears. I spot her up ahead, flung over Dad's shoulder. Tyler is mere feet behind them. I grin and sprint to catch up, knowing

I'll be inside her in mere minutes has an inferno of need warring inside me. Dad climbs the stairs to the back patio and rounds the corner where the hot tub is located. He drops Tess to her feet but doesn't step back. He grips her face and smashes his mouth to hers, she throws her arms around his neck and moans. Tyler and I both groan, then pull the cover off the tub. Tess breaks their kiss and gawks at the hot tub.

"Holy shit," she breathes out.

"Strip fast and get the fuck in before the water turns cold and we all die of hyperthermia," I growl. As if we are racing, all four of us begin tugging off our clothes, shoes, coats, hats, boxers and everything else, making it all sail through the air. Tyler is the first to jump in and groans at the feeling of the hot water. I grab Tess's waist and lift her in. Before she moves forward, Tyler snatches her away from me, walks her to the side and perches her ass on the edge.

"Legs open. You better come fast, hellion, or you'll freeze," he barks before he drops to his knees and buries his face in her perfect little cunt. Tess throws her head back and cries out at the feeling.

"Oh, fuck, Tyler. I'm so horny I'll come fast, I promise. Make me come on your face." Dad slips in the tub and moves toward her, she instantly reaches out and grips his cock in her hand and begins stroking him. Before he can seal his lips to hers she turns to me. "I want you, Kaiden." Like a slave obeying its master, I do as she says and hiss the second her dainty little hand wraps around my cock. Dad claims her lips while I suck on those perfect nipples that are as hard as ice.

ELEVEN

TESS

Oh, Jesus, send me straight to fucking hell.

If this is how good it feels to sin, then I am a fucking sinner. I'll own it and travel down south with a smile on my fucking face. Peyton was right, one man is cool but having three of them worship you like a goddamn goddess is next level.

The feeling of all three of their hot mouths on me is something I'll never be able to explain. The cold wind lashes at my back but the feeling is muted by the feelings they are drawing out of me. I break my kiss with Clayton and moan as Tyler swirls his tongue across my clit. I turn to Kaiden and capture his lips, needing to taste him. Clayton sucks on the tender flesh of my neck, marking me as his—*theirs*.

A shiver travels down my spine as I feel the

tension begin coiling inside me, my orgasm beginning to crest, but it doesn't even have time to build up before Tyler is forcing my climax from me. He sucks my clit into his mouth, making sure to scrape his teeth enough to throw me over the fucking edge.

I scream into Kaiden's mouth. He swallows every sound like they belong to him. Tyler pulls back and pushes to his feet, while Clayton and Kaiden each grab one of my legs and hold me open for Tyler. He doesn't go slow, he slams inside me with one hard thrust, forcing a sharp drawn out cry from me. Tyler's hand wraps around my throat and squeezes hard enough to apply pressure but not to restrict my airway.

"You take this dick like a good little whore, don't you, hellion?"

"Fuck yes," I pant.

"You like him fucking you, don't you, baby?" Kaiden coos as he bites down on my earlobe.

"Oh, shit. Tyler, just like that," I beg. Clayton reaches between us and circles my clit with his expert fingers.

"I want your cum to coat his cock, minx. Be a good girl and do as *Daddy* says."

Holy fuck!

Clayton referring to himself as *Daddy* hurtles me

over the fucking cliff like I am nothing but dead weight. This orgasm has no build up or even a warning before it slams into me like a tidal wave, robbing me of all logical thought, feeling and sight. I'm blinded for mere seconds as I soar like a fucking bird. As I come down slowly I'm shifted, forced to stand with my hands braced on either side of the tub with Kaiden sitting in front of me. He forces my head down onto his cock. I moan when Clayton spanks me.

"Fuck, I love this dirty little cunt," he growls before plunging inside me so hard I smack into Kaiden. "Yes, clench my cock like you own it." Without thought I do just that and clamp down on him, staking my claim over his dick.

Kaiden is forced from my mouth when Tyler shoves him over and directs my mouth to him while I stroke his brother. I alternate between them as Clayton continues to fuck me. "Close your eyes and don't open them," Tyler demands. I follow his instruction and relish in the way my senses overload without being able to see. I meant it when I said I wanted to be blindfolded and restrained when we fuck. Being at their mercy and completely under their control was something so out of this world.

"Fuck yeah, baby, suck his cock and swallow

every drop of his cum." Kaiden's crass words have me moaning around Tyler, whose fingers tangle in my hair tight enough to cause pain.

"Fuck!" he roars as he spills inside my mouth, forcing me to swallow all of his cum. I have no time to catch my breath before he is using his hold on my hair to force me onto Kaiden's dick. It sends a thrill of pleasure through me when Tyler keeps his hold on my hair and controls my movements as I suck Kaiden. "Oh yeah, hellion, swirl that tongue around my brother and make him beg."

"Yeah, baby. Just like that... You want me to come down your fucking throat?" Unable to answer I just moan my agreement. "Faster, Tyler," Kaiden snaps. Tyler obeys and yanks my hair, forcing me to move faster and bring his brother to climax. The second Kaiden's hot, salty release fills my throat I shudder. I greedily swallow every last drop of him, savoring the taste. A whimper escapes me as the taste of both brothers mixes across my tongue. I'm pulled free of both of their holds and am forced to my knees by Clayton. I flick my gaze up to him and relish in the sight of him stroking himself.

"Mouth open, you dirty little slut." I preen and do as he says but I poke my tongue out, needing to taste him. I clench my thighs together to dull the ache they have caused. Being able to taste father and sons at the same time is something I will forever yearn for. Clayton throws his head back and roars as jets of his cum hit my face and tongue.

Like a greedy little whore, I swipe my tongue across his cock, needing more of him. Clayton surprises me when he kneels in front of me and licks his cum off my cheek, only to grip my jaw and force my mouth open so he can spit the rest inside my mouth.

"Get the fuck up and get inside, Tess. I'm coming in your ass and cunt before I even think about letting you sleep tonight." Kaiden's promise has me shuddering with need.

"I want you to tie me up and blindfold me, then I want you to spit all yours and their cum in my mouth after you suck it out of my wretched little cunt," I growl. Clayton's eyes darken at my request.

"You're a filthy little cum slut, aren't you?" Clayton purrs.

"Only for you and your sons, *Daddy*," I answer.

TWELVE

TYLER

The time is flying by faster than any of us would like, the weather has started to ease and Thanksgiving has come and gone. The power came back on three days ago but none of us wanted to go back to our rooms.

Me, Dad and Kaiden have loved having access to Tess whenever we want. Sometimes one of us would wake up and fuck her, but of course, the other two couldn't let that slide, so we'd all take turns ravishing her tiny body.

Tess hasn't been able to take a single shower alone, all of us refuse to give her a moment of peace. This morning was one I will never forget. Dad was in a board meeting in his office over Zoom and Kaiden and I couldn't find Tess anywhere, so we thought we'd check his study. I couldn't spot her anywhere until Kaiden elbowed me and pointed under Dad's desk, where we could see Tess on her knees with our father's cock down her throat.

We of course had to punish her for leaving us out and we made sure to make her scream so Dad could hear. Serves that selfish fucker right for trying to hide her from us.

Each of us loves having her here. She has made this cabin come alive and breathed life back into it. During the days while Kaiden and I do some paperwork for Dad, she'll sit on the sofa and stare out the windows while typing furiously on her laptop. We asked her what she was writing but she refused to tell us. I tried to sneak a peek when she fell asleep but I had no chance at cracking her passcode.

Kaiden and I are sitting at the dining table, going over all the taxes for the family company to help Dad out while Tess is on the sofa daydreaming—the sight of her is distracting. She doesn't even have to do anything to get me hard. She just needs to breathe and I'm instantly hard for her. The shrill sound of her phone ringing shatters the silence. She jolts and quickly hunts around for her phone before bringing it to her ear. Kaiden and I straighten in our seats as we wait to hear who it is.

"Hey." She pauses to listen before speaking.

"Uh, yeah, I figured." She begins to nibble on her bottom lip, which we have learned is a nervous tick of hers. "Yeah. The storm has cleared and the snow has stopped." My stomach drops as a sinking feeling begins to overcome me. "No, I'm okay. I can just meet you back there."

She's leaving.

I spy Kaiden out of the corner of my eye. He's realizing the same thing I am, she's going to leave us and return to her normal life while we... remain here in the mountains without her.

Tess's tone drips with sadness as she says, "Yeah, I'll leave in the next day or so." I tune the rest of her conversation out, not wanting to hear it. Kaiden shoves back from the table and storms upstairs. Tess's eyes widen as she watches my brother stalk away. She ends the call quickly and peers back at me over the sofa. I don't have the strength to even muster a sad smile for her as my chest feels like it's caving in.

She opens her mouth to speak but I cut her off. "You're leaving?"

A whoosh of air escapes her and her shoulders slump. "I'm sorry, Ty—" I push back from the table and stand, forcing her to clamp her mouth closed.

"Don't be. You got your vacation and got to tick some sexual fantasies off your bucket list." Her face contorts in pain but I can't stop the words from spewing out of me. "Go back to school, Tess, at least the next guy you fuck, you'll have more experience now, huh?" Tears gather in her eyes.

"That's enough, Tyler," Dad snaps as he enters the living room.

"Whatever," I force out and storm up the stairs, only to nearly crash into Kaiden. He holds a finger to his lips. I roll my eyes but remain silent and listen.

"They're mad at me." Her tone is watery and I feel like a prick but I'm hurt, she's choosing to fuck off back to Rhode Island instead of staying here with us!

"They'll understand in time," Dad tries to reassure her. "My boys have never wanted for anything in their life. They have always been happy to live their lives here. No woman has ever been able to hold their attention for longer than mere hours. Yet, they find themselves wanting something you aren't ready to give."

"What's that?" she presses.

"More time," he says quietly. Kaiden and I both drop our gazes to the floor. Our dad is exposing our deepest wants and as much as I wish he wouldn't, I'm glad he is mature enough to do what we can't and communicate with her.

"I didn't mean for... all of this to happen, Clayton, I swear—"

"Shhhh." I can picture Dad wrapping his arms around her and holding her while she quietly cries. "None of this is your fault. There is no one to blame, we are all consenting adults, Tess. I guess my boys didn't expect to catch feelings for a girl who was supposed to be a guest of their brother's girlfriend. Now that they have, I'm afraid you won't be able to escape them."

"What does that mean?" Her voice is thick with anguish and I want to smack myself for causing her pain. I didn't mean to but she didn't pause or hesitate for a second to consider the idea of staying here with us.

"It means, I raised them to hunt. They know in order to survive they have to go after what they want and I'm afraid what they want is you, little minx. They may not be ready to admit that to themselves but when they are, they will come find you and force you to see them as something more than a vacation fling."

"And what about you?" she asks after a beat of silence.

"I've made my feelings for you clear before we even met. You have me for as long as you want me,

Tess, but I also won't force this life of isolation on you. You are still young and want to enjoy college, and if that is what you want, then I'll support that decision. If you ask me to wait for you while you finish school, I'll do it but it has to be your choice, not mine or my sons. You must want this life with us because from now on it won't just be me lusting after you, it will be them as well. We're now a package deal. I can already tell both my sons have fallen in love with you."

"They don't even really know me," she fires back, causing me to wince at her blatant brush off of our feelings.

"They know what they need to. You can't choose who you love, Tess. The heart wants what it wants. We are slaves to its needs and wants. You can spend decades with someone and never really know them. Sometimes you can spend two weeks with someone and know more about them just from observing. Don't underestimate them because I can promise you, they will continue to surprise you."

Tonight is the first night I have showered alone. Clayton told me he wouldn't be able to touch me or even pursue anything with me without his sons and I get it, but it also doesn't make it sting any less. I'm confused. I'm hurting because I don't know what to do.

When Peyton called earlier it popped the bubble I had been living in. I had forgotten all about the three of them being Van's family. They became... mine. It was just me and *my* guys but then reality came and shattered everything. Peyton told me they would have to reschedule their visit and come up at Christmas time. My chest constricts at the thought of her coming here and staying in this place without me. I never felt at home anywhere, not even in my childhood house but here... I feel like I belong.

A sigh escapes me as I step out of the bathroom and head to the room I was meant to stay in to change. The second I step inside the room, my eyes brim with tears at the sight of my bed. They brought my mattress up and made my bed.

No more sleepovers.

I close my eyes and inhale a deep breath. I made a mess of this whole situation but I didn't mean to. I never meant to hurt any of them but I also can't deny that I have a life outside of this place. I want to finish school—no, I need to finish school to prove my family wrong. I'm not some disappointment. I am smart enough and good enough to become a writer. I want to achieve my dream. I need to do this for me.

But is my dream worth losing them?

I push aside all thoughts of the guys. Before coming here I had one goal—finish school. It fucking pains me to think about leaving them all behind but I have to do this. I need to do this for me and if they can't support that choice, then they aren't the ending for my story. They may have been the climax, but that's it. I shouldn't have to sacrifice myself and my dreams for them.

With that thought in mind, I quickly change and

pack my things as I can't stay in this house. I can't bear the thought of them hating me and having to stay down the hall from them and not be able to touch them freely or even speak to any of them is killing me. I quickly open my laptop and compose a group email. I attach the PDF file and hit send before I can talk myself out of it. I quietly pad from my room with my bags in my hands. There's no sign of Kaiden or Tyler and disappointment wars inside me, but it's for the best. I can hear Clayton on the phone in his study and sigh. Fuck, I went and caught feelings for the priest's family.

Leaving them shouldn't hurt this much, it's only been a couple of weeks. Surely that isn't long enough to actually fall in love, is it? I close my eyes and pray for the strength I need to walk out of this door. I would love nothing more than to live out here with the three of them and build a life, but I refuse to lose myself in them. I have a dream and I plan to achieve that.

I dump my bags in the back seat of my car and slip inside. I know the second the car starts Clayton will come running. I keep my focus ahead as I start it, the engine splutters a couple of times before it finally roars to life. I plant my foot on the gas just as the front door swings out. I don't look back. I can't. The second I leave the driveway, my tears fall—I have fought them off since this morning but I can't contain them any longer. Horrible sobs rip out of me, it feels like my chest is splitting in half.

Clayton was wrong.

I don't think his sons were the only ones who went and fell in love.

I have never felt like this before. I've never cared about anyone before. This is all new to me and I hate it, this feeling is crippling and fucking horrendous. I never want to feel like this again!

I drove through the night, knowing if I stopped I would turn around and go back and give up my dream to keep them. Rather than head back to my dorm, I drove to Peyton's. I've been sitting in my car for close to forty minutes unable to gather the courage to get out and face my friends.

I'm scared they will judge me and call me a fool.

The last thing I need right now is for them to look at me with pity, I don't want their judgment or need it. When my phone pings with a message, I debate ignoring it in case it's Clayton or one of the guys, but when another message comes through I decide to check. I frown at the sight of Hudson's name and click the message open.

HUDSON

Get your ass in here.

Hurry up or we're cramming inside your car.

I smile even though I'm in agony, knowing that my friends have my back gives me the strength to finally climb out of the car. It's early hours in the morning and I know they should all be asleep. I don't dare to wonder why they are all up this late. Before I can even knock on the door it's yanked open and I'm met with the sight of Kye standing there in a pair of sweats and no shirt. The second he takes in the sight of me he growls, then yanks me against him and crushes me in a bear hug. Unable to stop my emotions from getting the better of me, I break down in his hold and cry.

Kye lifts me bride-style and carries me through

their home. I don't dare lift my head. I don't have the courage to face any of them, I'm too scared that they will judge me and worst of all, I can't face Van. How the hell do I tell my former priest that I have been riding his dad and brothers like I'm some rodeo queen?

"I got you, lil mama," Kye says quietly as he sits down with me in his lap. "I guess you had your heart broken, but just know Pey and the guys are here as well." I cringe despite my best efforts, I had hoped they would think I was just having a rough day or something.

"It's just me," Pey says when I feel a shift on the sofa. She reaches out and interlaces her fingers with mine. I muster the courage and lift my head to look at my best friend. One look at me and her face falls. "Oh, Tess," she mutters, then leans forward and wraps her arms around me as best as she can. This is the thing I fucking love most about Peyton, here I am sitting on one of her guys laps with his arms around me and she doesn't bat an eye at the position we are in. She knows all her men love her and she trusts them all unconditionally. She also knows I care about her guys, but not in that way, they are my friends.

"I didn't mean for it to happen," I choke out after

I manage to get my hysterical sobs under control. I wait to see judgment in her eyes or hear the guys scoff, but none of that happens. My best friend squeezes my hand and smiles sadly.

"I know what you mean, but sometimes we have no control over what happens or what our heart wants." She flicks her gaze over each of her guys and shoots them all a loving smile.

"I'm assuming you're broken-hearted because of my brothers and dad?" I slam my eyes closed at the sound of Van's voice. I wish I could say I didn't care what he thought but that's a lie. The last thing I want is for our friendship to be compromised because I fell for Kaiden, Tyler and Clayton. I feel like a fool but I still can't bring myself to regret anything that happened between the three of us. The memories we made together will be what keeps me warm on a cold, lonely winter's night. The way they made sure I was cared for, satisfied and most of all, I love how they always had to touch me. They may be men of few words, but their love language was touching and showing me they cared without needing to say it.

Pey shoots Van a look filled with warning. "Your tone isn't needed, priest," she bites out.

"And your mouth has better uses than telling me

off." Kye and Hudson both chuckle at Van's snarky remark.

Peyton rolls her eyes and focuses back on me. "Is he right?"

I expel a whoosh of air and reluctantly nod. "Yeah, he is," I answer quietly. "I didn't mean for anything to happen, I swear," I defend.

"Look at me, Tess." I fight back the urge to bury my face in Kye's chest and hide from Van. I inhale sharply and slip off Kye's lap to sit between him and Peyton, then slowly lift my head to look at Van, who is leaning against the wall with his tattooed arms crossed over his chest. How that dark angel was ever a priest is a wonder to me. His eyes hold an edge so I brace myself for his scorn. "Did any of them... force themselves on you?" he grits out. My eyes widen to the point I fear my eyeballs will pop the fuck out of my head.

"Van!" Pey scolds.

He shoots his girl a look that renders her silent. "I need you to answer, Tess," he urges in a tone that leaves no room for argument.

I shake my head. "No!" I force out through clenched teeth, suddenly angry that he would ever think so little of his family. "How dare you even think such a thing like that," I snap.

He scoffs. "Considering you're in my house, crying your eyes out without explanation and my dad and brothers have been blowing my phone up since you took off and refused to explain why they were so panicked, I'm kind of playing catch up here."

My nostrils flare in anger. "You want to judge me, then go right ahead, *Father Pierce,* but just remember those who live in glass houses shouldn't throw stones, huh?"

"Tess," I turn to Pey to see her features are pinched. I know this isn't their fault and I shouldn't be taking my hurt out on them. "Van is just trying to help. We all are, babe, but you kind of need to help us out here and explain," she pushes.

I scrub a hand down my face and wipe away the last of my tears. "Do you recall me telling you about a guy I was talking to online?" She pinches her lips to the side and nods. "Turns out, the older, single dad I was talking to is none other than Van's father."

"Oh shit," Hudson chokes out as he begins to laugh. Van glares at his friend before smacking him over the back of his head.

"Shut your trap, dick," Van hisses.

I ignore them as I push on. "I had no idea who Clayton was until I arrived at their home and saw him standing on the porch."

"You can take the girl out of the small town but you can't take the small town out of the girl," Kye rasps out from beside me. I scowl at him when he begins to laugh, then Hudson of course joins him, but when Van begins to shake with silent laughter I lose it.

"Screw all of you! I left that shit hole of a town and I never expected to shrink my pool of suitors when I joined that dating app. I mean, come on! Out of the millions of people in the US, I managed to match with Clayton fucking Pierce of all people. The world has a sick sense of humor, that's for damn sure," I clip out. To my horror, all fucking four of them begin to laugh. I try my hardest to fight against the urge to laugh but I lose the battle. Even I can see the funny side of all of this but my laughter quickly turns to sobs, then Peyton is there, holding me as I try to fight against my heart's reaction to losing the guys. For the first time in my life I finally felt like I belonged somewhere, only for it to blow up in my face.

FOURTEEN

CLAYTON

One week...

Morbid doesn't even begin to explain the feeling in our house. It's almost like the moment Tess left us in her dust she took all the joy and happiness we all felt with her. I've tried to reach out to her but she refuses to respond.

Tyler and Kaiden have been ghosts of their former selves. They haven't cracked a smile since she left, they barely talk and hide away in their rooms. I've spoken to Van, who told me she was back in Rhode Island but refuses to get involved and tell me how she is doing.

I can tell from the sharp edge to his tone that he isn't happy about the relationship we all developed but that is none of his concern. I stay out of his affairs so he needs to return that courtesy. He said they all still plan to come here for Christmas break, but when I asked if Tess would be joining them, he shut the conversation down by saying it would be just the four of them making the trip.

Kaiden is hurting but won't admit it, he's buried himself in helping me with work and fixing small things around the house to keep busy. Tyler has been holed up in his room. He does his part of the chores and work, but once he's finished, he retreats to his room.

"Tyler and I are going hunting. We'll be back tonight." I look up from my laptop to see my oldest son standing in the doorway with a grim look on his face. Kaiden isn't like Tyler, I can push Tyler to talk and express his feelings but not Kaiden—if you push him he'll just shut down.

"I'm pretty much finished for the day anyway. I'll come with you." He nods but says nothing as I stand. I quickly head to my room and change, meeting both my boys out back. Tyler hands me a rifle. I check it's loaded, then secure it to my back before nodding to Kaiden to lead the way. The snow is falling around us, covering our tracks. I raised my boys to never speak when they are in the woods. They know to howl if they need to make contact if we get separated. The fact the three of us are together and unable to speak is probably a good thing. I know they are blaming me for her leaving and I don't blame them. I will take their anger and blame if it means they will be able to overcome this loss.

I lie. Tess Cohen isn't someone you can ever get over.

We managed to get a deer. Kaiden has it strapped to his back. Tyler offered to butcher it while me and Kaiden wash up and prepare dinner. Honestly, I have no idea how to fix this fucked up situation. I wish I did, because I would give anything to take away the heartache my boys are feeling. I hate seeing them like this. I know there is only one person who can help them heal but she isn't here.

Showering even reminds me of her. The boys and I would each take turns washing with her so we could each get some alone time with Tess. I found myself looking forward to it each time, but now my shower just feels too big. I miss the smell of her apple shampoo and the feeling of her skin pressed against me. The sounds she would make as I slid inside her were euphoric.

"Fuck," I hiss. I'm alone in my shower with a raging hard-on, with only the thoughts of her to keep me company. I grip my cock in my hand and squeeze it... hard. A hiss tears out of me. I close my eyes and picture Tess on her knees, arms bound behind her with handcuffs, her eyes shielded by a blindfold.

"Fuck my mouth, Daddy," I picture her saying as I begin to stroke myself.

"Mouth open, you dirty little slut," I growl.

"Yes, Daddy." In my mind's eyes I can picture my cock slamming inside her mouth. The girl has no gag reflex and can take you down her throat without any effort. I imagine the feeling of her nails biting in the flesh of my ass as she pulls me closer, needing more. Last time we showered together this wasn't a dream, it was reality. She begged me to fuck her face.

I had reached down and squeezed her nose, cutting off her oxygen. She gasped around me and tried to get free but I refused, I knew she could take it. She took everything we gave her and still demanded more. Tess was a vortex, she sucked us all in. We were powerless to stop ourselves from falling for her. Sex with Tess is explosive, she never said no to trying anything and always trusted us.

I picture myself pulling out of her mouth and yanking her to her feet, before dropping to my knees. I love eating pussy and the fact hers is pierced only drives me wilder, wanting to taste her. I love the sounds she makes when we eat her rotten little cunt. I love the way she gets so wet and her juices drip onto my chin. I love being able to smell her in my beard hours later. Sometimes after I sucked our cum out of her holes, I could smell that as well and it drove me mad with need. Shrimping has been something I have always wanted to try and the fact Tess was willing to allow me to live out that fantasy, and not only try it but her loving it, was fucking exhilarating. My hunger for her is insatiable, if I could live inside her I fucking would.

My balls begin to tighten as the ghost of her taste assaults me and heightens my need to climax. My grip on my cock turns punishing, pain mixed with pleasure is what gets me off. I reach out with my other arm and brace it against the wall as I continue to thrust into my hand, with the memory of her screaming my name as she came on my face playing on repeat. I follow her over the edge, throwing my head back. I roar out my release with her name imprinted on my lips.

Aftershocks ride me hard, my knees tremble and my breathing is labored. I keep my grip on my dick tight as I wring out the last of my release. I press my head against the cold tiles as I finally release myself and breathe. The gaping hole in my chest only seems to widen as the loss of her hits me all over again.

"What the fuck have you done to me, little minx?" I grumble aloud. I try to push all thoughts of her from my mind as I quickly finish up in the shower. Once I'm changed, I make my way down-stairs and find Kaiden in the kitchen, peeling some potatoes. A frown mars his face. Normally I would leave him be and let him work out whatever is both-ering him, but not this time. "We should talk."

A growl rumbles out of him as he refuses to look at me, continuing on with his task. "What's there to talk about? We all got to fuck her, she left. No woman wants this fucking life. I'm good with that." He's normally a master at hiding his feelings, but not this time. I see right through his tough guy act.

"I call bullshit, Son."

He snaps his eyes to me and scowls. "Call it what you want but it doesn't change the outcome."

"You care about her."

He shrugs. "So what?"

I slam my hands down hard on the counter. "Then fight for her Kaiden!" I shout.

"I did!" he roars. "I fucking let her in. I let myself be fooled into thinking she was different and that maybe, just fucking *maybe*, she would see the beauty in living this life with us. But I was wrong. We're all destined to live this life alone and I'm okay with that. I have you and Tyler. I don't need anyone else." Hearing that come from my son, shreds my heart. Kaiden thinks he isn't worthy of finding someone to live this life with him, because his own mother abandoned him and chose to run away and live in the Big Apple.

"Son, Tess isn't *her*." I implore him to read between the lines. "She ran because we all couldn't accept the fact she had a life before us. She wants to finish school—no, she needs to finish school."

"Why?" he presses.

I sigh and run a hand through my hair. "She once told me her family turned their backs on her because she wanted more from her life than to be stuck in the small town she grew up in. She was supposed to end up with some boy she has known all her whole life, because that's what her mother wanted. Her finishing school is her way of showing her family that she is better than their expectations of her."

Kaiden's face contorts and I wait for him to work through his own thoughts. He needs to come to this conclusion by himself without my help. He needs to want this because I fucking *need* her and if both my boys can't face their own demons and realize the same thing, I'll have no choice but to give her up. I will sacrifice my happiness if it means my sons are happy.

I'd let Tess go for them and live my life as half a man, because without her I'm not whole.

"Tess, are you sure we can't convince you to come with us next week?" Peyton presses. I sigh and recline back in my chair, her and the guys have been trying to get me to change my mind about joining them for Christmas break, but the thought of facing Clayton, Kaiden and Tyler again makes me feel nauseous. I haven't heard from them since the day I left and honestly, I don't blame them. I gave them no explanation or a reason as to why I left. I thought they would have read my email by now and under-stood, but I guess I was wrong.

I shake my head. "Peyton, I can't," I whisper. Her eyes soften. Hudson slings his arm around her shoulders and draws her into his side. Jealousy surges inside me at the sight but I quickly tamp that bitch down. Van and Kye both smirk at them. I love how they all get along and none of them fight over her spending more time with one instead of the other. They have found a balance that works for them and I am truly happy for them but also, a part of me envies my best friend because I could have had that as well.

"The offer will stand regardless. You will always be welcome at our home in the mountains, Tess." I smile my thanks to Van, and stare down at my plate. I've been spending a lot of time here lately, being in my dorm room alone gives me too much time to think. I hate that I can't shut down and close my mind off from thinking about them. I hate how my body heats when I think about the nights I spent tangled up in them, or blindfolded with my arms bound behind my back at their mercy. I clench my thighs to try and dull the ache that is building. Just the mere thought of them sliding inside me or how their hands felt as they trailed down my naked flesh sends a shiver through me.

"You may not want to know my opinion but you're about to get it regardless," Hudson says, drawing my gaze to him. He leans forward and rests his arms on the table, a serious look overtaking his features and I find myself tensing in anticipation. "Love sucks." I gasp, the guys groan, while Peyton just smiles and shakes her head. I stare at my best friend, waiting for her to tell Hudson off or something but she just remains silent. "People will judge you for your choices but you know what the real test is?"

My brows slam together as I mull over his words. "No, what is the real test?"

He smiles smugly. "Proving people wrong. Love sucks because it takes control of you and forces you to obey without question. You can't fight against the pull no matter how hard you try. Just ask Pey. Her mother hates us being together and has pretty much cut her off, but none of that matters because we love each other. I don't give a fuck what anyone says or thinks about how we choose to live our lives. I don't fuck Lenior every night, I fuck her daughter, so her judgment means nothing to me and what others think shouldn't matter to you either."

I expel a loud exhale. "It's not about what people think or what they have to say," I admit.

"What is it then?" Kye presses. I roll my lips between my teeth trying to think of a way to explain, but Van takes the words right out of my mouth.

"My brothers won't leave the mountain. My dad won't leave them behind to chase Tess." His words have pain blooming in my chest. "She wants to finish school and I can bet my life on the fact that Kaiden kicked off when she mentioned something about leaving, then of course, Tyler got all up in his feelings and followed Kaiden's lead. Dad would have tried to change their minds but failed. So instead of coming after Tess himself, he chose to stay with my brothers because he won't let his happiness trump theirs." A stray tear slides down my cheek.

"I *need* to finish school. I have to do this, for me," I say as I run my gaze over each of them, then focus on Van as I finish. "I would love to live on that mountain with your father and brothers. The amount of inspiration I got just from being there was overwhelming. I would embrace their lifestyle and adapt if it meant I got *them,* but I can't do that without finishing what I set out to do. I..." I inhale and square my shoulders. "Your dad was right, it may have only been a couple of weeks but I love them, Van, and I wish I could go back there but I can't. I need to do this... for me." Heartache laces my words and I don't try to hide it. I'm done lying to myself and everyone else. I love Clayton, Kaiden and Tyler, and I miss them so fucking much that my chest aches.

"Well, I say tonight we need to get drunk until no one can see straight." Van's declaration is met with a chorus of hell yes from the guys. Peyton just sighs and nods. Hearing a priest say we should all get drunk is not something I ever thought I would hear.

"How can I say no to my priest?" she says to me.

I snort. "He stopped being a priest the moment he defiled our church when he fucked you in the confessional," I quip. The guys all burst out laughing, while Pey bites down on her lip and shoots me a sheepish look with a shrug.

"He's really hard to say no to, just look at him," she implores.

"She's been looking at my dad and brothers, bunny, she gets the raw sexuality of us Pierce men." Kye and Hudson both snicker and poke fun at Van, causing me and Peyton to laugh.

Drowning my sorrows in alcohol doesn't sound like such a bad idea.

I groan, my head is spinning and I feel sick. I have instant regret for agreeing to drink with the guys. I thought I could keep up and out drink them, but I think I may have underestimated their stamina. Peyton warned me not to give into Van when he kept teasing me and trying to get me to a play a drinking game, but I'm a sore loser and there was no fucking way I was going to let that asshole priest best me.

I'm an idiot.

A groan tumbles free when I roll over, trying to go back to sleep so I can sleep off this horrible feeling. When I hear the distinct sound of wood crackling, I tense. Peyton doesn't have a fireplace! I inhale, only to stiffen when the smell of a fire reaches my senses. I tentatively reach my arm out, hoping to feel it falling off the edge of the sofa I was sleeping on in their living room. My hand doesn't tumble off the edge, I just feel the empty space of a mattress.

I'm not at Peyton's.

The thought slams into me with such a force it knocks the queasy feeling straight out of me. I should open my eyes and confirm my suspicions, but I'm too much of a chicken shit. I could still be dreaming! I clear my thoughts and inhale again, only to be met with the same smell and the vacant space beside me. I give myself another minute to wallow in my self-pity before I allow the truth to sink in. Van and the guys set me up. I would bet money on the fact Van only baited me to get as drunk as I did so I would pass out and be none the wiser of him kidnapping me. The bastard had the hide to wear the collar of a priest and pledge vows to our good lord only to turn out to be a treacherous liar who backstabs his friends!

I'm back in the cabin.

Laying here in my room, staring up at my ceiling has become my favorite thing to do since she left. Every inch of this place reminds me of her except this room —we never fucked in here. Her scent doesn't cling to the curtains or the walls, it's the only place I can hide from the memories of her. I hear the ghost of her voice and laughter each time I brave leaving this room. Tess burrowed herself inside me and I hate it. I've never gotten attached before. I've fucked plenty of women in town and had no problems never knowing their names, or slipping out before the sun rose the next morning. I liked it that way.

I've never wanted to share this life with anyone. I love living in the mountains and never being burdened by a woman trying to make me choose between this place or her. My own mother couldn't stand living out here, I don't know why I thought Tess would be any different.

"Have you read the email?" I loll my head to the side to see my brother standing in the open doorway.

"What email?"

Tyler rolls his eyes and shakes his head, then moves toward my side table where my phone rests. He grabs it and inputs my passcode. I scowl at the little shit, no matter how many times I change the code he always figures out my pin somehow. When he finds whatever it is he is looking for he tosses my phone to me. I grab it and peer at the screen with a frown.

"What the fuck is this?" I press.

"It's the book she was writing for her English class while she was here. It's not finished." My brows hit my hairline at his answer. "The ending isn't complete, brother. There's a reason for that."

I focus back on Tyler and frown. "What's that supposed to mean?"

He shrugs and stuffs his hands in his pockets. "She can't write the ending without the three main characters. Read the book, Kaiden. Seeing our life through her eyes might help you understand her a bit better, and then you can finally let go of this anger so we can go after our girl."

I snort. "You and Dad can go right ahead and chase her, I'm not going anywhere."

Tyler scoffs and shakes his head in disappointment. "Read the fucking book, dipshit. You know very well Dad and I won't go after her without you. Don't make us lose the girl who stole all our hearts. I love you, Brother, but I'll never forgive you if you can't get out of your own damn way and see that she is meant for us and this life. We just need to be patient until she finishes school." Tyler doesn't wait around for a reply, he slams my bedroom door on his way out. I growl in annoyance. I want to toss my phone and ignore the email but the truth is, I'm desperate for some sort of connection to her again so I begin reading.

How do you fight the magnetic pull you feel toward three men? You can't, because they aren't something you can ever replace. They are a part of your very being, ingrained in your DNA, they are your reason for thriving and wanting more. I was never anything special in my small hometown. I didn't have the courage to chase my dreams or wants until I met my best friend who showed me it doesn't matter what your family thinks of your choices.

I left my town and enrolled in college. I thought that was as exciting as my life would get until I met a man online who set my blood on fire. He listened and heard everything I said. Never did he judge me for my choices. He was a stranger who showed me more compassion than my own family. I never thought we would actually meet until we did...

That moment didn't go as I pictured it would.

I snort out a laugh at the memory of her fainting in my arms and carrying her inside.

Not only did I meet the man who started helping me see I was worth more than my family had me believe I was worth, but I met his sons. Instant attraction doesn't seem like the right word. The three of them set me ablaze and forced me to embrace who I truly am.

Over Thanksgiving break I fell in love with not just one man but three.

My breath hitches as I reread the line three times, letting her words sink in. Hope begins to bloom inside me. I try to fight it but now that it's burning to life inside me, I have no choice but to allow it to consume me.

Not only did I fall in love with them, I fell in love with their place. I see a life here for the four of us. I want nothing more than to explore them and this place but I know I can't have my dream and them.

I hate that I have to choose because I want them with every fiber of my being. I want the life I know I can have with my guys in the mountains. God, I want it more than anything in *this world, but if I give in and stay, I lose my dream.*

If I ever get the courage to share this essay with them, I would tell them that I love them and wish more than anything that I could stay. I hate that I have to leave them in the mountains while I go back to the city. I'll never move on from them, I'm not who I used to be and that's because of the three of them. That they helped me see I'm worth more than some small town and that I can be more than I was raised to believe.

Society will judge us but I don't give up easily and I just hope they will see that—

I scroll and try to find the rest of the fucking story but there's nothing. I leap from my bed and rush across the room, then yank the door open, only to slam to a halt at the sight of my dad and brother leaning against the wall across from my room with their arms crossed over their chests.

"Do you see now, Son, that she didn't choose the

city life over you or us? She chose to go back so she could finish what she started because we all showed her she was more than some small town girl. We helped her believe in herself enough that she wanted to go back."

"I want her back, Dad," I grit out. A broad smile scratches across his face as he nods.

"Took you long enough, dumbass," Tyler adds. I shoot the shithead a glare that just makes him laugh.

Dad holds up his car keys and wags his brows. "Road trip?" he asks.

"Fuck yes."

"Hell yeah," Tyler and I both say in unison. The three of us all rush down the stairs. I side step Dad's mattress that's still in the living room as I grab my coat off the sofa and shrug it on.

"Are we expecting anyone?" Dad asks, drawing both mine and Tyler's attention toward the front of the house. I stalk across the room and peer out the front window to see headlights coming down the driveway. That bud of hope that was burning inside me is now a raging inferno. Tyler throws the front door open and steps out onto the porch with Dad and I hot on his heels.

I squint my eyes, trying to get a better look at the car, but it's too fucking dark. When the car finally comes to a stop in front of us, the hope inside me dies. It's not her car. When the driver steps out, my brows slam together in surprise.

"Van?" I rasp out. My brother smirks as he crosses his arms and leans against the side of the car. Another guy climbs out of the passenger side and moves around the car to stand next to my little brother.

"What are you doing here, Son?" Dad asks. He can't hide the happiness in his voice at finally seeing my brother after all these years.

Van shoots the guy beside him a look that has them both smiling. I clench my fists at my sides in irritation. "It's great to see you and all that shit but we have somewhere to be," I snap.

"Calm your tits, Tarzan. Jane is just fine," the fucker with my brother says.

"Who the fuck are you?" Tyler snaps, brushing his shoulder against mine, showing this fucker that we're ready to throw down if he makes another smart-ass remark.

"Both of you cool it, this is Hudson. He's Peyton's stepbrother." I keep my face blank of surprise at Van's revelation. "Considering both of us are going to have to grovel and beg our girl's forgiveness for what we just did, you both should show him some fucking gratitude, assholes." Tyler and I both reel back. Before I can go off on my little brother, Dad cuts in to try and diffuse the situation.

"What are you talking about, Van?" Dad asks.

My brother rolls his eyes, which just serves to piss me off. He and Hudson both step aside, offering us a clear view of the back door. When none of us says a word, Hudson groans and scrubs a hand down his face, then points his finger at me and says. "Tarzan." He shifts his hand and points at the back door of the car. "Jane is inside the car, passed out drunk. You're welcome, asshole."

It takes me a second to process what he's saying but when it finally sinks in, my eyes widen and my mouth parts in shock.

"Peyton is furious at us for getting involved in this shit but Tess is our friend, and I'll only say this once," Van warns as he runs his gaze over the three of us in warning. "If you hurt that girl or if this is just some fun for you all and you don't see a future with her, tell me now. Because if any of you break her heart, God won't be able to save your asses from me. Am I clear?"

"I appreciate what you have done for us, Brother, but respectfully, go fuck yourself." I snap my head to the side and stare at Tyler in shock. "She's ours. Your friend or not, Tess Cohen belongs to us, now hand her over."

"Looks like they have already stamped their claim on her," Hudson says with humor in his tone.

"She does have *Daddy* tattooed on her ass. I would say I definitely branded her as mine. Step aside, boys, and let us deal with her. We'll see you next week," Dad says as he moves down the porch steps toward them with Tyler and I hot on his heels. Van shoots us all a grin, the fucker is going to make sure we all know we owe him one after this. He may have been a priest but he has never been above blackmailing his siblings.

The moment dad pulls the door open and we see her lying there in the back seat passed out, I feel like I can finally breathe for the first time in three weeks. She looks beautiful. God, I missed her so much my chest begins to burn. How I thought I could ever go on living without her in my life is a fucking mystery to me.

Tess Cohen is ours and it's about time we made sure she knows that, because she's adding mine and Tyler's name to her ass as well.

SEVENTEEN

TESS

I take one last deep breath and slowly open my eyes, confirming what my mind already knew. I'm definitely back in the cabin. I inhale again and the scent of them wraps around me like a warm caress. I slowly sit up and scan the area around me ready to face them, except the place is empty.

My brows tug together in confusion as I slowly push to my feet. The buzz from the alcohol is gone thanks to my mild panic attack at realizing where I am. The only lighting is from the fireplace. I open my mouth to call out to them but then snap it closed when I see a note on the sofa. I reach out and grab it, turning to use the light of the fire to read it.

Need rips through me like a hurricane, my core clenching on air and I feel my arousal drenching my panties. We have a lot to discuss, but right now all I can think about is the feeling of all three of them filling each of my holes and stretching me out to fit them. I want them to punish me and call me a whore because for them, I am a whore. I can't get enough of their cocks and the taste of them.

My mouth waters as the ghost of their taste on my tongue haunts me. If they think I am going to give in and give them what they want, they are mistaken.

I rush down the hall into Clayton's office to retrieve the items I need, then run back into the living room. I strip down to my bra and panties, tossing my clothes onto the sofa before I kneel down on the mattress.

I grab the items I retrieved from the office and secure the black silk blindfold around my eyes, then grab the handcuffs. I do my best to secure my arms behind my back, then I wait. With the restriction of the cuffs and my sight gone, my other senses go into overdrive as I slow my breathing, listening for any sound. Goosebumps prickle my skin but it's not from the cold, it's from the heightened need thrumming through me. I know without a shadow of a doubt that they have been watching since the moment I woke up. Kaiden and Tyler are skilled hunters because they were trained by the best and I know they will come for their prey.

I'm ready to be eaten alive.

My breath hitches when I hear the back door open. I keep my head straight and don't turn toward the sound. My belly tightens with need as I hear footsteps approaching, my breathing turning ragged as the scent of snow, pine and raw masculine need perfumes the air. I may not be able to see them but I can *feel* them standing right in front of me.

"Would you look at that, boys. The whore is begging us without words to fuck her." The sound of Clayton's voice washes over me and I shiver.

"The slut disobeyed us, Dad." I squeeze my eyes tight at the sound of Tyler's voice—God, I missed the sound so much.

When I feel a calloused hand graze my cheek I gasp. "She wants to be punished for running away and taking our hearts with her." My lips part in shock at Kaiden's admission. "Yeah, baby, I didn't stutter. You belong to us, Tess, and we're going to remind you how good it feels to have our cocks inside you... then we'll punish you later for daring to run away."

"This time, when you run, hellion, we're chasing you and dragging your ass back here where it belongs," Tyler promises. Need roars to life inside me when I feel one of them slowly drag the straps of my bra down my arms. He yanks the cups down next, exposing my tits. When I feel his warm, wet mouth wrap around my nipple I throw my head back and cry out, only to be silenced when a cock is thrust inside my mouth. I gasp and begin spluttering at the sudden intrusion, but he doesn't give me a chance to recover as he continues to fuck my face, while the other continues to suck and nip at my nipples.

"You've never looked more beautiful, little minx," Clayton says, so it's Tyler and Kaiden touching me. I focus on the feeling of the cock inside my mouth and can tell from the size of him that it's Kaiden. "Get her on her back and show me her rotten little cunt." When Kaiden pulls out of my mouth, I suck in a ragged breath. I feel my spit trickling down my chin as they maneuver me so I'm on my back. My panties are ripped right off me, drawing a gasp of surprise from my lips.

"Fuck, she's soaked," I hear Kaiden growl.

"Let me clean her up. I need to taste her," Clayton says a second before I feel the mattress dip with his weight. Clayton doesn't tease me, he dives straight in, forcing his tongue inside my tight little pussy. My back arches as a shrill cry rips out of me. His hands grip my waist and hold me in place as he continues to tongue fuck me.

"Oh fuck, yes. Please, don't stop," I plead.

"You think you deserve to come, hellion?" Tyler growls.

I whimper as Clayton shifts and sucks my clit into his mouth as he begins circling my asshole with his thumb. "Yes! Fuck, I need it so bad, please." I'm mindless with need and will do anything they demand of me if they just let me have this climax. Fuck, I need it more than I need my next breath.

"I want her ass," I hear Kaiden growl.

"Her cunt is mine," Tyler declares.

Clayton pulls back, causing me to whimper at the loss of his mouth. "Tonight, I'm doing it right and sucking their cum out of you with a straw and you'll drink from my mouth. Am I clear?" My mouth falls open in surprise. I quickly snap it closed and swallow audibly.

"Yes, *Daddy*." The sound of them all groaning at my answer has a smile tugging at the corner of my lips. This right here is what I want forever—the three of them all at once, claiming me and marking me as theirs. I want them to dominate my body and use it to get off. I want to be everything they need and could ever possibly want.

My waist is grasped and I'm lifted, only to be turned so I am now straddling one of the guys. "Up," Tyler demands and smacks my ass. I press onto my knees and wait for him to line himself up with my entrance before I slowly begin sinking down onto him. Both of us moan and cry the moment I slam the remainder of the way down onto him. "Fuck, I missed this dirty little cunt, baby," he preens.

"I missed *you*," I respond without hesitation. A

hand lands between my shoulders and pushes me forward until I lay flat against Tyler. I hear the sound of something squirting and I know it's the lube. My pussy clenches in anticipation, causing Tyler to groan.

"She's getting wetter, Brother. She wants that cock in her ass *badly*," Tyler grits out.

"That right, baby? You want me in your ass, fucking you so hard I leave an imprint?" Kaiden's words cause an inferno to erupt inside me.

"Yes, I want all three of you. I need you to fill every one of my dirty holes and mark me as yours."

EIGHTEEN

TYLER

Her words have me twitching inside her. I meet Kaiden's gaze over her shoulder and nod. Tonight we'll give her everything she wants, then we'll punish her later for leaving us. I want to rip the blindfold off her eyes and look at her face as my brother slowly pushes inside her ass. Her mouth parts and a silent cry escapes her.

To my surprise she doesn't wait for Kaiden to sink the whole way in, she uses her upper body strength to sit up and slowly push back against him. He grips her chin and turns her face to the side so he can capture her lips in a kiss.

The sight of him kissing her and the feeling of her grinding down against me is almost too much. I fight off the urge to bust a nut as I reach out, pinching her nipples between my fingers. She breaks the kiss and cries out in pleasure.

"Dad, shut her the fuck up and shove your cock in her mouth," I snap. He obeys without complaint. He stands above my head, grips her hair and yanks it forward so she can suck him off while we fuck her. Kaiden draws back and slams inside her mercilessly. I grit my teeth and drive upward, meeting him thrust for thrust. She moans around Dad's cock as we fuck her.

Her spit starts landing on my naked chest as she swallows Dad as deep as she can. "Fuck yes. Suck my cock like that as my sons fuck you like a whore," he coos, thrusting into her mouth. Kaiden and I find a rhythm and within seconds, Tess is trying to release Dad so she can scream as her orgasm ploughs through her without mercy. Her screams are muffled. Kaiden wraps an arm around her waist to keep her upright as tremors race through her at a rapid speed. It's like her orgasm has set us all off and the need to follow over the euphoric edge compels us all to thrust deeper, harder, just so we can fall into oblivion with her.

"Fuck, yes. Just like that. I want you to swallow every drop, then you can taste them once they are done," Dad says in a strangled tone. Two thrusts later and he's roaring out his release, forcing Tess to swallow every drop. She does without complaint and moans as she does it. I've never met a girl who loves to swallow before—Tess is an anomaly and I fucking love her. I'm so head over heels in love with her it's unhealthy.

Dad pulls back and growls his approval as he runs his fingers down her cheek, then quickly disappears into the kitchen. Tess may love shrimping but it's not something I ever plan on trying.

"Fuck, yes, baby. Push back on my cock just like that and make me come," Kaiden grits out through clenched teeth.

"Fuck, Tyler, I need you to fuck me harder. I need to come with you both." I lock eyes with Kaiden and as if an unspoken vow forms between us, we make it our mission to get our girl to come one last time before we empty everything we have inside of her. Our thrusts are hard and unrelenting as we chase our release. "Oh, God, yes... like that, please. Keep fucking me like that," she screams as Kaiden and I slam inside at the same time. Her cries of pleasure are music to our fucking ears, we follow her over the cliff of euphoria, her name a prayer on our lips as we come. Aftershocks are still wracking through her body as Dad reappears and nods to us both. Kaiden and I ease out of her. I feel cold without her body heat against me. Dad makes quick work of pushing her onto her back and forcing her legs open. Kaiden and I both stare at him as he pushes a straw in her ass and sucks out my brother's cum.

I shudder at the sight when he shifts up her body and pushes the other end of the straw in her mouth. I watch in sick fascination as her throat bobs as she swallows. Once she has taken everything, Dad yanks the straw free, then pushes it inside her pussy, sucking *my* release out of her, only to repeat the same step. Kaiden and I say nothing as we wait for them to finish *shrimping*.

Dad tosses the straw to the side once she has swallowed every last drop, then smashes his lips against hers. She tries to tug against her restraints and that snaps me into action. I race into his office and retrieve the keys. Coming back, I kneel down beside them on the mattress, forcing Dad to break the kiss as I gently help her into a sitting position and release the cuffs. She shucks her bra off the remainder of the way, then brings her wrists in front of her and massages them. Kaiden kneels down on her side and slowly reaches out to remove the blind-fold. She blinks her eyes a few times, adjusting to the light, then runs her gaze over the three of us. The silence in the room is so loud I almost choke on it.

"I'm sorry," she whispers. I jerk in surprise, that was not what I expected to come out of her mouth. Dad reaches out and cups her cheek. She nuzzles into his touch, bringing a smile to his lips.

"You have nothing to be sorry about," he says.

She opens her mouth but Kaiden cuts in before she can speak. "We were idiots. You have every right to want to finish school." Her brows bunch, forcing him to reach out to smooth the indent between her eyes. "We'll be here supporting you, baby."

Tears shine in her eyes. I grip her chin and force her to focus on me. "We'll come visit you at school and you can come here on breaks. We'll make this work, Tess." A lone tear falls, I swipe it away with my thumb and press my lips to hers in a soft kiss.

"We will do whatever it takes to ensure you pass college and visit. We'll move to the city until you finish school if that's what you want," Dad says quietly, but I can hear the hint of hope in his tone. None of us want to lose her and the fact we are all willing to give up our life here, and work remotely in the city until she graduates, shows that she means everything to us.

She darts her tongue and moistens her lips.

"What if..." She clamps her mouth closed and swallows audibly. "What if I switched to online classes?" she offers.

"No." All three of us turn to Kaiden in surprise. Tess's face falls and she drops her gaze to her lap. I'm two seconds away from knocking my brother out. Kaiden reaches out and forces her head up to meet his gaze—even Dad is glaring at him. "You deserve the full college experience." Her eyes widen in surprise. "We love you, Tess, and if loving you means we have to stay in the city for a couple of years, then so be it. We can always come back here on your breaks, but I won't let you give up college for us."

Tears fall from her eyes and I begin to panic that Kaiden just ruined this for us until she laughs, then launches forward and wraps her arms around his neck. He melts into her. "Thank you," she chokes out. She pulls back, then hugs Dad, and then finally it's my turn but a hug isn't enough, so I claim her lips in a kiss, showing her without words that no matter what it takes we will ensure she achieves her dream and we will be by her side every step of the way. Her family may not have been able to see the greatness and the bright light that she is, but we did and we will do everything in our power to make sure her light continues to shine fucking brighter than all of the stars.

"I need to hunt. Get the fuck up and run, baby. We're chasing you down and fucking like a rabid dog this time." Tess stares at Kaiden with her mouth slightly ajar.

"It's cold out," she protests weakly.

"We'll fuck the warmth back into you," Dad adds.

"But—"

I cut her off before she can continue her weak ass protests. "Shut the fuck up and do as you're told, you slut, and run." Her eyes glaze over with need. She leaps to her feet and snags my coat from the back of the sofa, then slips her feet in Kaiden's boots before rushing out the back door.

"Let's go hunting for pussy, boys," Dad says, causing us all to laugh. We're not just hunting pussy tonight, we're hunting our future.

Two years later...

I have one year left of school and I can't wait to be done. Peyton is feeling the same. Well, I mean I'm over school because I want to go home to the mountains full time—she's just over it because she's pregnant and can't see her feet anymore.

"I swear, I am going to kill them for making me fat." I choke on my latte as I whirl around and stare at my best friend.

"You aren't fat. You're having a baby!" I scold. She waves me off and I roll my eyes. Peyton is still acting like she is not about to pop and bring life into this world. Her mom has cut her off for good now and it hurts me to see my best friend go through that, but when my own mother reached out to me I was shocked to my core. I thought for sure she would cut me off when I told her I was engaged to three guys, but she bit her tongue and asked if I would be bringing them home to meet her. I nearly died on the fucking spot. My guys and I are planning a trip back home next week. Pey and her guys are joining us.

"It's gonna be weird going back there when Mom and Ken aren't together anymore," she mutters beside me as we walk outside of the science building. Ken and her mom are now separated. Ken refused to cut Hudson off and Lenoir couldn't handle that, so Ken asked her to leave. He supports Hudson and Peyton and their choices, at least they both have their dads in their corner.

"I know, right? I can't wait to meet the sister that has taken over the church. I wonder if she is as nasty as the last priest?" I snicker. Pey laughs and shoves me.

"That poor girl has no idea that we ruined that church."

I snort. "I wonder if Clayton and the guys would be down to defile it some more?" I ponder.

"If it involves me being inside that pussy, then I'm down, baby." I whirl around at the sound of Kaiden's voice to see Tyler, Clayton, Van, Hudson and Kye all standing by a nearby tree. Peyton just huffs and shakes her head.

"I can walk home without the three of you escorting me," Pey snips out. Her guys all chuckle and ignore her anger as they stalk toward her and kiss her hello, just as mine do the same. The stares of the other students used to bother me but not anymore. Clayton wraps his arms around me from behind.

"Don't be mad at my son and the boys, P. He just wants to make sure my grandchild is safe and I for one am totally on board with that." Peyton sighs and melts slightly at Clayton's words. Much like her own dad and Ken, Clayton has been nothing but supportive, and the fact they have no idea which one of them is the father makes it so much sweeter that all their fathers love that baby without care.

"Right, well, my brother's ugly face is killing my mood so let's go, babe," Kaiden says, earning a glare from Van.

"You and *our* brother fuck the same girl dipshit," Van snaps.

"And? Our dad fucks her too and I don't see him complaining. We got the good looks and you didn't so that's why I don't mind looking at Tyler while I'm fucking Tess from behind." I groan and cover my face. Ever since Clayton and the boys moved here full time three months ago, because none of us liked being apart, Van and Kaiden have done nothing but bicker and fight daily. I can't wait to finish school and move back to the mountains. God, I miss our cabin and the dirty things we got up to. I miss running around naked through the woods and getting fucked against the trees.

"You're an overbearing ass. Tess doesn't even like you," Van hisses.

"She has mine and Tyler's names tattooed on her ass as well as Dad's. I'd say our girl likes us just fine, right, baby?" When he swings those puppy dogs eyes to me I can't help but melt. I shoot Van my best I'm sorry look that has him grinding his teeth.

"Yes, babe, I love you and now I need you inside me, so can we go?" All three of my guys mutter an apology, then I'm being thrown over Tyler's shoulder as they march us out of the school and toward the car.

This is my life and I fucking love it! I got my dirty daddy and his sons. I won the fucking jackpot.

I hope so because hot fucking damn, Daddy and his boys had me panting!

Thank you so much for reading Dirty Daddy, I fucking loved writing this book, truly. I have always wanted to write a pure smut book and I finally got the chance to do that.

I cannot thank you enough for reading *Dirty Daddy*, it means the world to me that you have taken a chance on reading one of my books!

ACKNOWLEDGMENTS

Marcus, my dirty daddy. This book is for you. Your disco stick will always have me panting and wanting to run through the woods naked in the snow just so you can rail me against a tree.

MJ & Ray-Ray, my loves. I pray to God that you both never read this acknowledgment because that then means you read this book and fuck that. This book is not for you, my darlings. Please forgive Mummy for being a dirty mofo!
Leah, my evil minded twin. I fucking love you and can't thank you enough for forcing me to write these books because I am in love with this whole world.

My PA, Sarah–My Queen–Wilson, the ship would sink without you, babe. I am so in awe of you and can't thank you enough for all the hard work you do. I don't deserve you xxx

Alex Denver, I fucking love you for allowing me to use *your* tattoo inspo for this book. I hope you loved Daddy, babe!

My alpha's, Debbie, Clare, Erin and Samantha, you ladies are the core of this whole thing and without your nasty ass input I don't think Daddy would have been this nasty with his shrimping.

My beta babes, Taay, Amber, Amanda, Nicole, Patti, Morgan & Rizzo, I fucking love you crazy ladies. Thank you for being on this dirty ass ride with me.

My ARC army girls, thank you beautiful souls so fucking much for always sticking by me and trusting me to mend those hearts that I break.

Lizz, none of this would be possible without you! I can't put into words what you mean to me, my friend. I am so grateful for you and all that you do for me. I love you xxx

My darling dark delicious readers, thank you again for following me and reading each of these books. I know I break your hearts and leave you mad when I end a book on a cliffy, but I love that you trust me enough to heal those hearts and come back for more. I love you.

Sam xxx

Mafia Romance

<u>Murdoch Mafia Series</u>

Played By The Bishop

Tormented By The King

Tortured By The Knight

Tempted By The Queen

Turned By The Pawn

Ruined By The Rook

<u>Murdoch Mafia Novella</u>

Stalemate

<u>Memento Mori Series</u>

Reign Of Royal

Broken By Sin

In Havoc Lays Chaos

<u>Godfathers of the night</u>

London has Fallen

Damned By His Angel

<u>Re Della Strada</u>

Shattered Soul

Fractured Heart

Tainted Essence

<u>Fairytales With A Twist</u>

Condemned Beast

Secret Society/ Bully

Filthy Few

Forever Filthy

Filthiest Of Them All

Masked Men Novella (Pure Smut)

Dirty Priest

Dirty Daddy

Sports Romance

<u>Playing For Keeps</u>

Offside

Touchdown

End Game

Hail Mary

Blindside

RH Sports

Hate Us Like You Mean It

MM

Love Me Like You Mean It

Paranormal Romance

<u>The Veil Of Obsidian</u>

Of Time And Carnage

<u>Curse Of Fate</u>

Dream

Fate

Nightmare

Redemption

Anarchy

<u>Brutal Savages</u>

Savage Lies

Brutal Truth

Savage Beast

Brutal Beauty

ABOUT THE AUTHOR

Samantha Barrett is originally from Auckland, New Zealand but living in Brisbane, Australia.

Sam writes all things dirty dark and delicious with a side of twisted mind fuck.

She is a lover of all things red flags and an anti-hero is a must.